Shattering Worlds

C. D. Tavenor

Shattering Worlds by C. D. Tavenor

Twitter: @tavenorcd

Published by Two Doctors Media Collaborative, LLC

www.twodoctorsmedia.com

contact@twodoctorsmedia.com

ISBN: 978-1-952706-10-3 (paperback)
ISBN: 978-1-952706-12-7 (e-book)

Cover Graphics

File ID 160238436 | © Alteraposto | Dreamstime.com

Shattering Worlds

A SciFi and Fantasy Story Collection

C. D. Tavenor

Foreword

Thank you for diving into *Shattering Worlds: A SciFi and Fantasy Story Collection*. If this is your first time reading any of my stories, welcome! I'm glad you're here. For those of you returning to my words, welcome back.

In *Shattering Worlds*, you might recognize a few places, characters, or locations found in my other work. Some of these stories are adaptations of chapters or ideas that didn't make it into the final product of my other novels. A few might feel completely linked to those stories.

I'll leave it up to the reader to decide whether those stories actually occur in the same universe. You'll just need to wait and see what happens next in those worlds.

Without any further delay, though, please dive into *Shattering Worlds*. May you explore new planets, meet new friends, and uncover fantastical realities from across the spectrum of the SciFi/Fantasy genres.

From Fear, Find Fire

Shintau. The gutter of the Shendari Empire. No one goes there, unless they're going somewhere else. Or to die.

Pebbles crackled beneath Selina's feet. Sprinting down Nactur Alley and away from Old Vincent's Bakery, she looked over her shoulder, spotting the large man chasing with a rolling pin in hand.

"You bastard girl!" He barreled into the crowd she'd just dodged. "If only your mother could see you now."

Selina leapt over a sludgy puddle, vaulted the gates surrounding Bhan's warehouse, and slipped through one of its wooden doors just as it closed at the heels of a worker. Sliding behind one of the large rows of platted shelves, she ducked into a shadowy corner. Satisfied no one noticed her sneak inside, Selina reached in her pocket, revealing a scarlet heat-shard, one of her most prized possessions. With a push of Fire, it glowed, and within moments it was lightly toasting the bread in her hands. A minute later, she bit into the loaf—the first warm food in over a week.

Vincent may have known mother, she thought, *but he has no idea what she'd think of me.*

Like everyone else in the abysmal city of Shintau, he hadn't been there when Selina's mother died. He hadn't heard the words she'd said, lying sick in bed. "Selina, you are strong. It kills me to leave you, but I know you will survive. You're a McEntyre. Find Henrietta, and she'll keep you safe."

Problem, though. Who was Henrietta? And just hours later, her mother passed without any further explanation. *So Vincent can say mother would have said otherwise, but mother said I'm strong. That I'll survive. That I'm a McEntyre.* She emphasized that fact. *I'm a McEntyre, not a Thentir.*

Selina took another bite of the bread. Its airy, humid warmth drowned out the rest of her thoughts. It tasted like cake, if cake lacked sugar. It was the greatest morsel ever devoured. After a few minutes, she finished her meal and pocketed the heat-shard. Fortunately, Vincent seemed to have missed the Bhan warehouse in his search for her.

From the shadows, Selina watched the movements of the workers as they located goods to ship to far away cities. A few stood near her hiding place, but she'd used this little enclave of wood for weeks. No one ever noticed her. The next worker passed on his way toward a row filled with wine barrels—her opportunity to slip back outside. Wiping the crumbs from her ragged blouse, she sprinted out of the darkness, reached the door, and pulled the handle. Exiting into Nactur Alley, she headed back toward the bakery, hoping Vincent was still off searching for her.

Quite the mistake, she realized, for as she neared Market Street, Vincent was leaning against his rickety sign, speaking with three guards.

His green, hawkish eyes immediately noticed her. "There she is," he said, wagging his finger toward the alley. "She might be only fourteen, but she'll slip right through you! Get her!"

Selina dug her heels against the cobblestone and began a new flight through the city. This time, she headed straight for the market. Sprawling beyond Vincent's bakery, a maze of tents and shacks blended into an amalgamation of vendors, con artists, and merchants of all shapes and sizes. In Shintau, denizens could just as easily find a shard smith from Fendari as they could meet a Chankor silk weaver. But it was Selina's home. She'd always lived in Shintau. She knew the streets better than anyone else.

Green tent flaps whipped behind her as she barreled through Carlo's jewelry stand. The man gaped as she rolled over his table without touching a single ounce of gold. Around apple farmers and butchers and tailors she ran, the smells of the market complimenting the bread filling her stomach. The only flaw in the flight came from the shouts behind her—the swordsmen in Shintau-purple were gaining even as she somersaulted over a water barrel. *These seasoned soldiers could run!*

She darted around a wooden cart selling pastries and shot down a long grassy lane between rows of stalls. After a few steps, she slipped between two tents, nearly pulling the cloth down around her. She paused, watching two soldiers run by, and then a third. A sigh of relief arrived, but the feeling was short-lived, for their boot falls clanked back toward her respite.

She pushed further into her ill-fated hiding place, and as the third guard arrived, drew his sword, and faced her, she lifted the tent cloth, sliding inside an unknown shop. She had just a second to notice the screams of a tailor measuring a half-naked man's waist before she was back into the light. Down another grassy lane, she arrived at a brick wall, found its iron gate, and entered the fisherman's ward, cordoned off from the rest of the market for its obvious—and salty—stench.

Jogging past two or three stalls, she chanced a glance toward the wall, noting the soldiers hadn't passed through the gate yet. Slipping behind a massive wagon loaded with trout, she spotted her target.

Andrew. Right where he ought to be.

He was skinning a tuna, ripping its scales into a bloody mess on his table. Casually walking across the muddy lane, she slid behind his stall and tapped him on the shoulder.

"Andy, glad I found you." She bit her lip, staring up at his eyes.

"Selina!" He dropped the knife to the table so suddenly, it nearly fell off the wood toward his foot. "Uh, what are you doing here? Good to see you, though."

The rustle of chain-mail alerted her to the arriving soldiers. She had no time to explain, no time to justify, she just acted. Leaning forward, she grabbed his mussy brown hair and pulled his lips toward her own, kissing him. Out of the corner of her eye, she watched the three guardsmen round the corner. They weren't going to pay any attention to two silly children kissing on the job. They walked right past Andrew's fish fest, heading deeper into the market.

After ten long seconds, she released the kiss. He stared at her, dumbfounded.

She winked. "Thanks," she said, heading in the opposite direction of the soldiers.

"You're welcome?" Andrew replied, though she didn't glance back.

* * *

During the day, Selina enjoyed the warmth and openness of the streets of Shintau. At night, she retreated to a place few wished to visit. Along the cliffs of northern Shintau, overlooking the Sea of Storms and Serpents, tiny stones adorned a flat expanse of grass, bushes, and tree stands. To the east, an unfinished ditch reeked of decaying embalmed flesh. Gazing upon the lethal ocean, the mounds of stones symbolized the unmarked graves of the dead.

Beneath a willow, Selina pretended her mother's body was buried in the earth somewhere nearby. She knew it was probably in the mass grave over the ridge, but she avoided considering that truth. Here, at night, Selina found safety, away from the prying eyes of Shintau's underworld.

Yet as she found safety, she also found fear, dread, despair . . . and ice, destroying her soul.

A particularly cold breeze blew in from the north, and far out at sea, lightning flashed inside the perpetual storms plaguing the waters. Sometimes, she imagined the sea serpents leaping beneath the electric blasts, their endless dance sending a clear message to any sailors who wished to venture too far from shore. Tonight, she saw nothing, only her shadow shivering amidst the icy chill echoing through her bones.

Slowly, she gathered a bundle of sticks fallen from the great tree above her. Beneath the tiny pyramid of twigs, she placed a few dry leaves, crackled from the day's blaze. She had no flint, but she could push flame from Soul—and her heat-shard. At least, on certain days. *If it's too cold, I always fail.*

While reaching out for Soul, she placed her hand above the tepee while holding the heat-shard in the other. The brown leaves were aching for energy to explode their dried veins. Soul tugged at the strands, urging them to accelerate until excitement overwhelmed and ignited in flame. Yet today, power eluded her. *Why? I literally heated a loaf of bread this afternoon. And no fire tonight?* Today, on a day when she needed comfort more than ever, she couldn't tap her power to bring forth warmth. The failure made the iciness of the air all the more chilling.

After a few extra minutes, the effort took its toll. Her eyes drooped in the face of the blistering wind threatening to destroy her bones. Smashing her makeshift fire with her fist, she slid against the trunk of the tree. Between two roots, she pulled her knees close. The evening would hurt, but it wouldn't kill her. *I think.*

Closing her eyes, she prayed to an unknown god—any god—for a dreamless sleep. Solace didn't arrive. Instead, the voices drowned her.

You are worthless. No one loves you. Your mother left you. Your father left you. You deserve no one, for you are no one.

Throw yourself from the cliff. It will end the pain. Join your mother. She wishes to see you.

Just end the pain. Join the crews. Let them use you. It's better than this.

She wanted to scream, but instead, she bit her lip, a trickle of blood dripping toward her chin. She tried to pull forth the words of her mother, the words that gave strength during the day, but the night smashed the thought like a bug.

"I thought, against all odds, I might find you here."

A voice crashed through the darkness. Painfully alert, Selina sat up.

Blocking the moon, a shadow of a man looked down upon her. "It's time you came home."

A second, then she recognized the voice. "Papa?"

"Selina, this is no place for a Thentir. I expected to find you at Henrietta's, but you're here. Why are you here?"

Tears streaked down her face. He'd found her. The thought was both terrifying and joyful at the same time. She remembered the smiles, yet she also remembered the bruises. Blood. Bile.

But her bones were freezing, her arms aching. Her tongue was dry, parched for water. The man above her held out his hand, and she reached out, taking it. It was soft, it was warm—his tendrils wrapped around her consciousness, whispering *welcome home.*

* * *

Potatoes. Inside the bowl, beneath the floury porridge, her spoon crushed the familiar chunks of solid potatoes. She remembered the chowder her father would make them, spiced just right with black pepper and garlic. Lifting the spoon to her crusty lips, she tasted the soup, letting its heat overtake her throat. Its aromas overwhelmed.

"Like you remember?" he asked.

"Mmmm," she mumbled through the viscous liquid filling her mouth.

"Good. So when did she die?"

They'd sat at the table for two minutes before he asked the question she dreaded. "Why's it matter? She's gone."

He raised his hands in placation. "I only heard yesterday. I've been looking for you since then. Knew you'd need a bed."

Selina slurped the chowder, swallowing before finding the next few words. Maybe this time, things would turn out differently. "She died about a month ago. Doctor suspected it was the pox."

"A month? And Henrietta never picked you up?"

That name again. *Why, for the life of me, can I not remember who she is?* "I don't know. Guess not."

"Hey, look at me when you speak."

Her eyes lifted, expecting flames, but instead—kindness, in his face. He cared. Somehow, he cared.

"Well, you're Selina Thentir, you're my daughter. You're a survivor. You've done well. And now . . . we're reunited. We'll head west; forge a new life in the Reach. In Fendari, or beyond."

After another sip of the chowder, she dropped the spoon into the bowl. He'd called her a Thentir. That wasn't her name. That was his name, but it wasn't *her* name. *It wasn't Mother's name.* "My name is Selina McEntyre. I'm not going by Thentir."

With those words, she stared at her chowder, but she stole a glance further up the table, seeing his knuckles resting. Tightening. Further still, his buttoned green shirt. Reaching his eyes, she saw pain. Fear. Yet also . . . hope?

"No, you're a Thentir," he said. "You're with me now. I know you loved your mother, but I'm the only one who can take care of you. So you'll wear my name."

I should say yes. She should accept his authority, thanking him for his sudden hospitality after his distance over the past year. Yet she remembered the moment her mother cast him out of the house. "You're a fool, and you better never step foot near us ever again," she had said, bolstered by the strength of the two spirit healers standing by her side.

"No," Selina said, her eyes truly meeting his for the first time. "My name is Selina McEntyre."

And with that line, her father's steeled fire ignited. His eyelids hardened, his eyebrows creased. Her earliest memories returned, awaking in her crib to the screams of her mother from the room over.

"You will obey me," he said, and he swiped the bowl in front of her off the table and into the barren wall. "This is my house. You're my daughter."

She stood, feeling not only his anger but her own. "This is not your house. It should be my house. Her house. You were forced to leave our house. You abandoned us. And then our house was overtaken by a gang when she died. And all this time, you had this house?" The emotions, though having disappeared hours earlier, rose within her, fighting to escape and unleash their power upon the world. Yet in response, a cold embrace enveloped her—it was him. He was assaulting her with a tendril of Soul entirely beyond her comprehension. Everything was cold. She couldn't move. Her legs locked; she fell back into her chair.

"Don't you think your mother tried to burn me, too?" he said, rising from his chair. "Do you really think you can beat me? You are mine."

Selina shrunk into a ball. Her back was against wooden planks, and his power—oh, his power—quashed all her hope for a moment where she would draw upon a push of Fire, meager as it might be. Instead, she used her only remaining tool. She screamed.

The sound released from her lips for a mere moment, but its blood-curling shriek sliced through the air dividing them. He stared. He understood. And he swung his right arm, smacking her across the chin.

Selina flew to the dirt floor, crumpling into a heap. Through the window, the moon's white light contrasted against the orange flames of hell emanating from behind her father. He was practically anointed by rage, his spirit tendrils revealing his true self. She crawled toward the door.

But seconds later, he grabbed her by the neck and lifted her, slamming her onto the table. "You're just like your bitch of a mother. Always resisting control. Never accepting the truth. I am in charge. You are my daughter. You *will* do as I say. You—"

The door slammed open, the force fracturing and reverberating throughout the shack. "Thentir, you asshole, get your hands off that girl."

Somehow, Selina lifted her head, her line of vision reaching just over her chest. Standing in the doorway, a tall, dark-skinned woman pointed a flintlock pistol straight at her father. Her black coat contrasted with her white shirt, but the ice in her eyes exuded a ferocity never before shown by either of her parents.

"Oh, what makes you think you have the right ta' tell me what to do? Where the hell have you been?" But as he said the words, her father stepped away from the table, pressing himself against the wall, the woman's weapon eviscerating his will. His pale skin blushed in terror.

Selina, frozen with fear, remained on the table, watching the scene. Her brain searched for an answer, seeking a name for the woman before her. *I know I've seen her before, in some distant recess of my memory.*

"You thought you'd get away with beating her like you beat her mother? Did you think I wouldn't find her? Just because I'm gone for months or years at a time doesn't mean I won't visit my best friend when I return. That doesn't mean I don't know where to find you, even when you try to hide in your shadowy lair." The woman whipped the pistol toward Selina's father, its wooden handle cracking into his ear. Blood splattering against maple logs, he crumpled to the floor.

His concentration finally fracturing, Selina discovered an ounce of strength, pushing herself up onto her elbows. Horror spread across his face. His true self wasn't one of rage or power. It was simply one of fear, projecting his own insecurities onto the two women who should have been his family. The two women he should have loved.

"Selina," said the large woman, "are you all right? I'm so sorry. This never should have happened. I should have been by Theodora's side."

Only now did Selina hear her own breathing, releasing at a rate unnatural for most. She slipped off the table, falling to the dirt. Her eyes met her father's, but they'd glazed over, his composure reduced to rubble.

The older woman leaned down, still holding the gun with its barrel pointed toward the crippled man. "You poor, poor thing." Her hand gently rested against Selina's cheek.

Selina wanted to feel its warmth, but the world was black. "My father, is he all right? Will he be okay?" The words came naturally to her mouth, though they tasted like ash.

"That man, that man right there? He is not your father. Never has been."

Not her father. She considered the words. She thought about the fists and the claws, the scratches and the scars obliterating her mother's flesh. She remembered the moments when he disappeared for weeks, claiming he was off on business. But Selina knew. She'd seen him visit those secret places deep within the slums, where scum exploited men and women trapped in squalor. Scum like her father.

Yet . . . he wasn't her father.

She pushed herself up from the ground with a little hop, her feet landing lightly on the dusty floor. The power previously evading her reach rushed into her soul, revealing every molecule in the room. Henrietta stepped back, most likely sensing the tempest raging within the girl—no—the woman, facing her tormentor.

"You aren't my father," she said, enveloping the man in a blanket of heat, intent on searing his skin. Towering over the crumpled man, she found the void behind his pupils. His emptiness. She recognized it, the same helplessness which had overpowered Selina since her mother died. The man was terribly—and justifiably—alone, especially in this moment. *If I smite him, I'm no better than the shell of a man he's become.*

She released her connection to fire magic. His skin glowed a faint red, but nothing more. "You aren't my father," she said again. "You never were."

A hand rested on her shoulder, and she glanced up at her savior—Henrietta. Selina noticed the woman's woven dreads draping from her hair, and a faint memory returned from years ago, throwing a ball with her mother and a friend. This woman.

"Thank you for finding me," Selina said, taking a step toward the door.

"Do you have any things we need to collect?" asked Henrietta.

"There's nothing here I want," she said. "It's time to go."

The Coast Guard

Ben was strong enough. He understood the truth. They deserved this. He deserved this. The world deserved this. His parents should be proud—he was making the world a better place, one sacrifice at a time.

Rather than giving him strength, the thoughts washed an alien heat over his body, and Ben nearly lost balance before his hands grasped the ceramic edge of the sink. Bile rushed through his throat, emptying his stomach of the protein portion eaten for breakfast.

Waving a hand in front of the faucet, a ration of water trickled, washing away the moist crumbs. Ben took a sip from an already-filled cup and spit, phlegm landing squarely on a brown chunk struggling to slide down the drain. Reaching for the towel hanging on the wall, he wiped his face. He breathed. He breathed again.

Knots in his stomach unraveled, but the enveloping silence continued to deafen Ben's soul. He wanted to curl up under the covers and watch an episode of . . . *something*, even if leading into the night he most likely wouldn't have electricity. Electricity. He hadn't been alive when they started rationing energy alongside food and water. The clouds outside shadowed the room through the skylight, yet it wasn't time to activate biolights.

The subtle misting of rain broke through the background, like the light buzzing of a bee hidden in a garden. If only they'd saved the bees—

He needed to stop stalling. They deserved a swift end, now that they reached it. He had to go outside and face the future. With one final breath, Ben walked out of the washroom and through the small cabin serving as his quarters. After acquiring them from his closet, he looped a yellow sash over his emerald uniform and placed a red beret on his head. When he opened the door to leave, the change in air pressure thrust a half-written letter from the tiny desk onto the floor beneath his feet. A moment of weakness—he'd never say the words.

His boots clicked against the linoleum of the hallway. He headed toward the exit, alone—everyone else had already reached their positions. He was the only one who rushed to seek relief after the final hour of orientation.

Pushing open the door, he exited into the dreamy mist. The immense Hudson Seawall spread northeast in all its glory, from Middletown to Long Beach. The massive steel bulwark rose out of the water, expansive walkways adorning either side of its central parapet. And distributed evenly along the mechanical levee, from shore to shore, hundreds of metal frames rose upward in semi-circles. Beneath each loop, at least two or three individuals dangled, their hands chained to the top of the hoop. Their knees knocked against the iron platforms. In front of each set of prisoners, Ben's fellow guards read the final rites.

Walking along the temporary catwalk dozens of feet above the waves, he stared straight ahead, not bothering to make eye contact with any comrades. From the water below, he tasted a tinge of salt, though not unexpected, given the circumstances. As murky, oily waves crashed, spray splashed upward, stinging his face. The Coordinators warned it might singe skin if they weren't careful, though a tiny burn was a small price compared to the greater cost spent today.

Another knot tried to rise in Ben's stomach, and he squeezed his thumb against his index finger, cracking at least two knuckles. Passing the fourth concrete parapet, he caught the tears streaking down the face of an old man, wrinkles indicating an age of at least seventy or eighty years old. He might even remember the end of the twentieth century. Why did he cry? He didn't deserve sadness. It was his fault—their fault—they were here today. Ben hated all of them for bringing us to this point. Why couldn't they have done something? Anything? Instead, they'd forced the lottery upon themselves.

Though, they shouldn't be scared or upset. The lottery: the greatest honor any citizen of the Coastal Republic could receive, whether participating as a guard or as a sacrifice. Of course Ben had volunteered.

Passing beneath the next parapet, he neared a sign reading CARSON. Before the prisoners came into view, he stopped, leaning his hand against the nearby concrete. Damp from the misty rains, he nearly doubled over, cramps hitting his sides. Ben knew he *could* go through with it. He'd recited the laws. The rites. The charges. He knew them by heart. Why did pain continue to strike?

He brushed water out of his eyes, stepping around the tower. Tied beneath the swaying sign, a man and a woman slumped, reaching for each other as the rain slapped their brown skin. The woman's hair, white against her black jumpsuit, whipped with the ocean wind flowing toward New York. At the sound of footsteps, the man looked up, icy anger breaking his defeated gaze.

"Benjamin!" he shouted. Unnecessary—Ben could hear fine from ten feet away. "Why? Why are you doing this?"

Ben stopped in front of them. "Connor Carson. Harriet Carson. I have arrived to read your eulogy." He strained against the urge to consider more than his role.

"God damn it Ben," Connor said. "Look at her! She's broken. You've broken her. Is this what you wanted? Is this the best way to change the world?"

Ben ignored the words, but he thanked the precipitation from the clouds above. If tears washed his cheeks, they wouldn't notice. He turned south, toward the distant ocean. The splendor of the sea spread outward, the shorelines peaceful. If only the future looked similarly calm. It wasn't calm, because . . . because of them.

Speaking with enough force and without facing them, Ben said, "By the order of the Miami Accords, you have been sentenced to death for your crimes against Earth, against the atmosphere of this planet, and against the entire human species. Under the rights vested in me by the Constitution of 2041, I speak these final words to condemn your life to the waves."

Ben glanced up and down the seawall, watching others speak toward the ocean, too. Did they feel the same anguish? Or did they want to keep their eye on the horizon? He didn't know. Did it matter? But *they* felt pain.

Good. And . . . Ben felt pain, too. Also good.

"Look at me in these final moments, boy. Look at her in these final moments."

Compassion pulled at Ben's soul, but he resisted the urge to turn. They didn't deserve it. He didn't deserve the moment, either. They'd thrown the right away years ago. When they deceived him, telling him if he ate only plants, everything would be all right.

"Because you were born prior to the year 2010, you are eligible for condemnation by the Last Generation," Ben said, ignoring the plea. "The lottery has selected you as a necessary sacrifice. Remember that *your death*, allowed by your contribution to *the death of this planet*, ensures your children, your grandchildren, and all future generations to come, will have the chance to flourish upon this planet as you did. Through each death, we eliminate one more mouth."

A torrential downpour plowed into the wall, and Ben raised a hand to wipe water from his eyes. Just as quickly as it arrived, the sheet disappeared. Straightening his back, Ben hardened his thoughts. He needed to finish the ceremony. Every second made each word that much more difficult. Still, he waited, wondering if the man would say another word. And her silence . . . it drilled into Ben's brain from beyond the pattering of the rain.

"First count." Ben urged his neck to turn toward the prisoners, but a higher power resisted. "You, the Millennial generations, you knew what caused climate change. You knew the risks. You did not act. Your negligence condemns you."

"Yes we did!" cried a voice. Ben thought for a moment it was hers, but it came from somewhere else along the wall. Amongst the cacophony of voices reverberating throughout the bay, no one could replicate Harriet's sound.

Ben closed his eyes. "Second count. When report upon report emphasized the risk, your generation continued using the poisons of the world. Gasoline. Airplanes. Cars. Natural gas. Coal." His mind shifted to the simple things, and he deviated from the memorized script. "You even kept the lights on when you left the house, and drove to work when you could have biked!" He sighed, looking down the line. One of his comrades frowned; Ben refocused his words. "You voted against the climate, because you thought, *the world isn't ready for change,* or *we'll make the change next week, but not now.*"

A whimper sounded from . . . from her.

"Third count. You hid behind the cardinal sin, the cardinal excuse. You said, *it's society's problem, not mine. We must fix society, and when we fix society, each person will shift their behaviors.* Yet you used the excuse as a pretext not to act on your own volition, not to encourage those around you to reject the poison, not to ensure your children had a planet to enjoy." The tears streamed down Ben's cheeks, anger radiating. But they knew he believed every word he said. He hoped they believed the words too, for their sake. For his own sake.

"Fourth count. You recognized the crimes of past generations, yet instead of holding them accountable, you partook in the same excesses created by their resounding commitment to unsustainable growth. Rather than reject it, you hypocritically paid lip-service to the future while embracing the same sins."

"Benjamin, we did none of these things!" said Connor, breaking the silence Ben had hoped would persist for eternity. "You know this. You know we believed in a better way."

Remembering dinners from long ago, conversations swirled in subconscious memories. Shouts at the TV as another politician pushed back the date of decarbonization. Critiques of the new Constitution and its implications. Rejections of the post-UN Charters and the Eco-Education Programmes. Had they really believed in a better way?

"Fifth count." Ben opened his eyes, the words drying in his mouth. He could not say them. He could not tell his parents, without looking at them, their greatest crime. Ben pivoted on the iron catwalk, facing the two who raised him. Who coddled him for thirty years, somehow *assuring* a future. Who held him when the fifth hurricane in a decade struck New Jersey's coastline, killing three thousand people. Who turned the TV off as ten million died in a Bangladesh epidemic following the fracturing of their levees.

"Fifth count," Ben said, staring down Connor and Harriet Carson, mother and father of Benjamin Carson, the man he was. The man he despised. "You failed to educate the next generation of your mistakes. You continuously failed to act, you continuously failed to do what was necessary to stabilize the planet. You failed your children, your grandchildren. And the greatest crime of all? You failed to recognize that even if *you* did not fail, the failure of *your peers* does not absolve you of guilt."

He exhaled, releasing fists he hadn't known he'd clenched. Pain and anger and sorrow and terror bellowed from his skin like steam from a tea kettle. The Coordinators predicted this moment would come. He needed to embrace hate in order to finish the final rites.

Yet Connor stared at him. Ben. Their son.

The old man's eyelids fluttered, fracturing his anger. He drooped, as if he wished to flatten his body against the steel, but his bindings tugged him back to his knees. Ben knelt three feet from their faces, rain plastering the space between them. He tried to meet their eyes. Hate wasn't the only path available.

"I have made peace with my choice," Ben said. "When I submitted your names into the lottery, I thought you'd understand."

Connor didn't look up. Harriet continued staring at the ground, though Ben thought one of her eyes glimmered. Most likely a tear.

Once again, Ben deviated from the script. "You serve a higher cause. Indiscriminate elimination of the generations who failed to save the planet. Through your death, we ensure a better world. You know why the Miami Accords were established. You helped negotiate them. Did you not expect the next generation to follow through? You think we like this? You think we're enjoying this? Your generation failed! Your generation made us do this!"

"We made you do nothing," said fath—Connor.

Ben stood. Fire burned throughout his heart. They'd failed to accept the truth of his words, and their failure stoked the flames of anger devouring his mind. He wasn't wrong. They had no other option. If Ben's generation was to save the world for their kids, for their grandkids, and for *their* grandkids, sacrifices must be made for the greater good.

Ben wanted to strike them. He wanted to force them to submit. His arm rose into a swing, but he looked to the left. His comrades began the long walk, leaving their offerings behind. They had done their duty without breaking. Ben could too.

"I love you, Connor. Harriet. I forgive you. But I won't back down from what's at stake."

"I know you won't."

Ben's eyes widened. In these final moments, she . . . she spoke. Her eyes were blazing with warmth and power. She bored straight to the deepest recesses of his mind, to the parts not darkened by never-ending peril. The wrinkles on her cheeks were drenched in rain-soaked tears, yet somehow, she stretched her lips and smiled.

"My boy, Benjamin," she said. "I love you. And I forgive you too. Do what you must."

Ben's heart shattered. His knees quivered. He wanted to hug her, embrace her, he wanted to hear him say the same words. At the same time, the urge to strike them remained tensed in his forearms. She faced her fate with more bravery than the one holding the noose around her neck.

Connor glanced at her, a tiny smile breaking his lips. Her strength must have invigorated him too. "I don't forgive you," he said, "but if she can, she forgives for both of us."

The man probably desired to hold his wife in these final moments. But Ben couldn't give mercy. He stood, turning his back on them yet again. Deep at sea, lightning struck, sheets of rain pounded the waves, and pitch-black clouds swirled in a tempest of power destined to strike New York with fire and fury. The perfect executioner—a storm like this one only existed due to the folly of a runaway greenhouse effect. Killed by their own creation.

Ben considered the unfinished letter remaining in his room. Looking back toward them, the words he'd explored adding to its end sprung forth, escaping his lips before he could stop himself. "Thank you. Your sacrifice will be remembered."

With those final words, their eyes turned to the sea, looking past Ben, past their son, toward Superstorm Victor, the harbinger of their sacrifice. Through its waters, through its winds, through its surge, the ocean would decide their destiny. For a moment, Ben joined them, staring beyond the horizon and toward their fate. It was the fate of his generation, too. As it descended into darkness, its only hope of escape was to dive straight through the eye of the hurricane, hoping to find the quiet beyond.

More likely, it would kill them too, Ben knew.

He didn't look back as he turned in step with his comrades. He joined the long line heading toward the North Jersey Processing Facility. Above the doorway, a massive digital screen read:

> *You have served a higher cause in your contribution to the Seventh Lottery of the Coastal Republic of the Americas. In this year, 2054 C.E., we will remember your sacrifice.*

His sacrifice, or the sacrifice of his parents? Saltwater mixed with Ben's tears. The wailing and gnashing of the failed generations, chained for their collective crime, finally numbed his consciousness. Did the Coordinators think Republic citizens were happy they sacrificed the lives of their parents to save the world? Anger bubbled in Ben's soul. All of humanity forced their hand by its past actions. Why couldn't they have given them another way?

His mother's words replayed in Ben's mind. *And I forgive you too.* She didn't hate him. She understood the terrible choice he made. Perhaps everyone else would too. Perhaps even his father, when fate arrived in the night. Ben pitied them. They were victims of a system they'd lacked the strength to break. The next generation had broken it instead, even as it continued to crack them to the bone.

Ben reached the end of the catwalk. The immense swirl of white, grey, and black dominated the horizon, the storm mere hours from landfall. Its waters would rush the bay, thrashing the Hudson Seawall. The Coastal Republic's path into the future might not be the only way, but it was *a way*, and they'd made their peace with it.

* * *

Or so Ben thought. He awoke in the middle of the night to a cold sweat. Heart racing, pulse pounding, his eyes fluttered. The bio-light in the ceiling faintly glowed a dim purple, the algae releasing its luminescence. Through the tiny barred window, lightning flashed. He couldn't hear the thunder, nor the rain, but the storm had arrived. They were in its midst.

His parents were in its midst.

Feet sliding to the floor, he instinctively grabbed his coat and headed out the door. His roommate silently snored, sleeping as if a thousand people weren't about to die outside. The adrenaline of the day faded, his mind calmed. What they were doing was *wrong*. And there was nothing Ben could do to stop it.

Yet, there was something he could do to give himself peace.

Tomorrow, he and the other guards would have the task of defending and saving the city, even as the storm continued ravaging the coastline. They'd search for people in their homes, bring supplies, and repair what needed repaired. All the while, they would forget the souls abandoned on the sea wall.

No, Ben wouldn't forget them. He was going to join them.

Reaching the end of the hall, he arrived at the door to the outside. Through the tiny glass porthole, water plastered the wall with a lion's ferocity, shredding and tearing into the concrete. After zipping up his coat, Ben placed a hand on the secured door handle, twisted, and pushed it open into the wind.

It took all his strength, but the outside opened, and he slid onto the sea wall. Under a pitch black night sky, he couldn't see the shape of the hurricane above, but the guide-lights on the wall illuminated the sheets of rain rolling in from the ocean. And the wind—the wind! Its power rocked his bones. Still, he pressed onward, pushing through the rain and down the wall past already-murdered corpses.

It took him far too long to reach the Carson tomb, but when he arrived, he found their mangled bodies hanging from shackles. He was too late. He couldn't join them in their deaths.

No. Wait.

Ben leaned over, seeing the shallow breath of Harriet, his mother. Her chest rose and fell, slowly, though her eyes were closed. Over the roar of the rain, he whispered, "I'm here, mother." She was most likely unconscious, but he didn't care. He'd stay with her until the end. Until both their ends.

Pivoting, Ben stared outward into inky blackness, facing the unseen torrent assaulting the great metropolis at his back. Hurricanes were the natural cleanser of sea, the tempests which gain power from the waters beneath and unleash fury upon the land. Even before the climate crisis, humans feared the hurricane. When the temperatures and seas began to rise, they only worsened. Superstorm Victor, out there somewhere—or directly above him—was supposedly one of the worst ever.

Ben grimaced, the wind ripping at his skin. "I give myself to you! Alongside my parents. If I can sacrifice them, I can sacrifice myself! It's only fair."

Silence, of course, other than the already persistent roar of the waves. He didn't know what he expected, except to die, but a few final words made—

With a crash, a wall of water smacked into him, throwing him past his mother and father and over the Hudson-side of the wall. The thrill of icy air flushed his hair, the water below rushing to meet him. What a way to end.

A chance second later, he crashed into the frigid water. His shocked mind embraced the darkness and the cold, all-encompassing relief he hoped would come from death. At least his mind was at peace.

But death did not arrive.

Ben floated in the water, suspended. He *knew* he should be dead. If the cold didn't kill him, if he didn't drown, the toxic slime mixed in with the water would burn the skin right off his bones. Instead, Ben felt . . . peace. A new awareness crept through his system, one of serenity and knowledge, as if he were being greeted by a friend always present but never known until this very moment.

He swirled beneath the choppy surface of the bay. He breathed—and instead of drinking in murky water and flooding his lungs, his body breathed in the liquid like it was simply air, as if he had always breathed like this. Every droplet was for the taking. Under his control. He felt alive—ready to become what he was always meant to be.

Now it was time to discover that truth. He had sacrificed himself to the tempest, and the tempest had welcomed him with open arms. He would become its servant, guarding the coast in a way he'd never imagined.

Ben smiled, kicking his feet into motion. The waters around him cleared as he swam by, as if his presence willed decades-worth of pollution to separate and flee in fear.

A new reality awaited. He only hoped he wasn't too late to craft it, honoring his parents' sacrifice with every remaining second of his life.

For the Empire

"What do you have to say for yourself, Adralis?"

The cold copper stings the skin around my wrists and ankles. Lifting my chin, I look up at the Iron Bench. Three justices stare at me, their silky white hair running past their shoulders. Their eyes are all an icy blue, and their nearly translucent, crystal-white skin glimmers in the dim candlelight of the courtroom. They've set me on a wooden pedestal, making it impossible to touch the rocky walls surrounding us.

"Are you willing to listen to my tale?" I say. "I stand by my actions. I have only ever served our people."

The three judges glance back and forth, imperceptible messages passing between their eyes. After a pause that feels like an eternity, the leftmost one says, "We grant you the opportunity to testify on your behalf. You may present your case."

I swallow. The lump in my throat feels like a rock. "Thank you, your honors. I will not disappoint you."

"Of course you won't," says a voice from behind me. The High Inquisitor, of course. A rock floats over my head, landing on the table in front of me. "Touch the seeing stone. The truth shall set you free."

* * *

It was a cool evening in the town of Geropolis, and I was making my rounds, visiting the poor. As a deacon in the Order of White, it was my duty to assist the least fortunate, providing them with food, clothing, and sometimes shelter. In the back of our monastery, we had beds available for those who needed them, and every night, they overflowed.

Above my head and surrounding the town, the marble pillars ascended into the sky. Their immense, rocky bulks haphazardly blocked the sun at random parts of the day, clouds shifting and misting between their sheer peaks. To some, they represented the demons of the underground striking toward the heavens. To me, they represented peace, prosperity, and a reminder of home. But I don't need to tell you, justices, what they represented.

Walking through the market, I heard the shuffle of feet from a nearby alley. The footfalls sounded barefoot, and my mind began to churn. Only the impoverished ran without shoes, and it had been some time since a pauper lived so close to the market. I approached the shadowed side street, and moonlight faintly reflected off the eyes of a young boy tucked behind a dumpster.

"Hello there," I said, beckoning with my right hand. "I've not seen you in town before."

The boy scampered further into the alley, but I followed him, unafraid. Thugs knew to avoid members of the Order of White. "I won't hurt you; I just want to make sure you're okay. I have food. What do you need?"

It was at this moment I felt the calling in the back of my mind for the first time in five years. It echoed through the stones at my feet. Powerful, given my skin wasn't touching them. My eyes widened, but I held back my soul from immediately responding. I was not in a safe place to receive a message.

In the meantime, the boy scampered forward, nearly crawling on all fours. Beneath his disheveled hair, his eyes frantically darted back and forth in fear. "You said food?"

"Of course," I said, reaching into the basket held in my other hand. I tossed him an apple. "What's your name?"

Catching the fruit, he took a bite, and his cheeks rose in joy. "Muh na'es Char'ie," he said between crunches.

I returned to the market, and he followed closely on my heels. In the brighter space, the dirt on his face was visible, smeared from ear to ear. A torn tunic hung limply on his spindly limbs. I dropped to my knee, and as it touched the cobblestone, I felt the call once again—it felt more urgent than before. I needed to hurry, but I had time.

"Well, Charlie, my name is Adralis Vas Karath." I pointed at my silver hood. "Do you know what I am?"

The boy shook his head. I figured he was from out of town. "I'm a monk. We help people. We help kids. We can take care of you." I held out my hand.

He stared at me pensively, and for a second, I was unsure if he understood what I was saying. But from around the corner of a nearby street walked a guard holding a long pike. His red feather bounced as he trotted toward us. I sighed.

"Your eminence," said the man, probably fifty years my junior. "Is this miscreant bothering you?"

If he weren't so young, I'd have found him attractive. I waved my hand lazily in the air, noticing Charlie cowering between us. "Oh bugger off. This boy's not hurting anyone."

"You know the rules, though. If he's not with you at the monastery after curfew, he's in violation."

"Well, he's with me, isn't he?"

With that comment, Charlie scooted subtly toward my leg. Good lad.

"All right then," said the guard. "I better not find him on the streets alone."

As the snobby red coat sauntered away, I held out my hand again to my new friend. "Come on," I said. "Let's go."

He reached up, and I pulled him to his feet. Silently, we paced through the market, up the hill on the north side of town, and to the Hall of Wisdom, the building holding the Order of White. Looping around through the back courtyard, we reached the old barn now doubling as our homeless shelter. Leaning against the open door, Xenia was chewing a leaf.

"Ah, Adralis," she said. "And who do we have here?"

Charlie took a final bite of his apple before chucking it toward the side of the barn. "I'm Charlie," he said. "He saved me from a guard."

"Adralis will do that," she said.

"And he needs a place to sleep." I patted him on the head. "Found him in an alley behind Mercer's Tavern, and guards were prowling tonight."

"Where are you from, Charlie?" asked Xenia.

"Uh, I don't know," he mutters, shaking his head.

With those words, a migraine struck my brain, practically splitting my forehead wide open. There was powerful magic at play, if it was reverberating through the soil. "Xenia, can you take it from here?" I pressed my thumbs above my ears.

"Yeah, of course, you all right?" she asked.

"I'm fine, I just need to lay down."

The calling echoing with each footfall, I rushed beneath the stone archways of the monastery and made my way toward my rooms. Entering, I took a brief swig of water from my pitcher to wash away the pain. Satisfied, I kneeled at the foot of my bed and whispered the words, "Gar'lak El'in Tal." I haphazardly pricked my finger with a knife, rubbed the blood between my hands, and placed my palms on the marble tiles beneath my feet. Blackness enveloping, I slid into the void and *through* the rock, its warm embrace welcoming.

"Adralis Vas Karath," said a voice. High Inquisitor Tarik. "You have taken too long to answer our call."

I responded in kind, a wordless message billowing up from my soul. "My lord, I had to ensure I reached a safe place before answering your call. I could not arouse suspicion in the middle of town."

"I do not wish to hear your excuses. Accept the rebuke and move forward."

Cringing, I nodded, unsure if he could detect the motion through our blood bond.

"I accept your admonishment, my lord," I said. "What does the Inquisition wish of me?"

"For these past thirty years, Adralis, you have served the Empire well. Very few have infiltrated an Order so successfully. They truly believe you are one of them."

"They embrace me," I said. "I have proven my worth time and time again, and they do not question my convictions. You taught me well, my lord."

"Yes, yes, spare the flattery. You don't need to prove your allegiance."

I closed my eyes, though the High Inquisitor could not see me. "As you wish. What are my orders?"

"When we last spoke, you informed us of insurrectionists in the forests surrounding Geropolis," said my lord. "Do those rebels still persist to this day?"

I racked my brain for the requested data. "They aren't as strong as they used to be, given the bolstered military presence around the city, but they're still there. Given the right opportunity, they will strike, even after half a decade of bandit tactics."

"Good. Then here are your orders. Within the next ten-day, the governor of the Province of Aurelia will arrive in Geropolis. You will assassinate him, and await further instruction."

"Your will shall be executed without question," I said, instinctively speaking the ritual words. "I am an instrument of the Empire upon the surface of Eda."

The darkness faded, my lord ending our connection. I shifted out of the comfort of rock and back into the open air of my quarters. Sweat dripped down my face, arms, and legs, the power of our blood bond sapping at my bones. I flopped onto my bed, instantly falling asleep.

* * *

The next five-day, and then the next, passed without incident. I fed children and paupers in the barn alongside Xenia and our colleagues. Charlie gained a new light, his eyes glowing while gaining strength. Yet on the ninth day after the High Inquisitor contacted me, we received word Governor Richard Theas of Aurelia would arrive the next day. And he arrived, taking residence in the mayor's villa on the far side of town.

That night, I rolled out of bed. From my window, the moon was nowhere to be seen, and dark clouds blocked starlight from reaching the ground. With the words "Rela Las Tin" and a firm grip on a piece of granite, darkness became day in my eyes. I leapt through the window.

It was in these moments—when I was fully enthralled in our power—that my mind remembered our home. At least once a month, I took time to traverse the wilderness in full form, touching every rock I could see. I knew the rules; I never approached the pillars. But from afar, I worshipped them, for they reminded me of home. Of all of you. Of the Empire. And so I confess. On that night, before I executed my orders, I crouched atop the roof of the Hall of Wisdom. With my eyes now accustomed to the dark, I looked from mountainous pillar to mountainous pillar, embracing each one, praying they would give me power and strength. I hope you forgive me for failing to execute my mission immediately. I missed our people.

After my minutes of reverence, from shadow to shadow I shifted, sneaking through the alleys used by those I served. My black cloak hung closely to my legs, and my silver hood changed with the colors of its surroundings, its camouflage taking effect when necessary. Within an hour, I reached the south side of town—where the wealthiest residents lived. Glowing lights danced from the windows of the mayor's house, indicating a party still raged late into the night. Approaching from the east, I vaulted a sandstone wall, crouched beneath the rose bushes of his garden, and climbed a gutter to the top floor.

I waited.

The hours passed, and I almost believed the party would reach dawn, but then the torches extinguished, the final guests walking through the gate. I gave the governor thirty minutes to fall asleep before I approached the edge of the roof, found the window to the master suite, and slipped through, landing on ceramic tile. To my left was a door. To my right, an immense bed, surrounded by silk drapes, dominated the room.

I approached the bed, and as I got closer, I heard slow moans. Of course, the governor was using someone for his pleasure, and suspicions rebounded through my skull. My inhibitions lowered, I brushed aside the bed's cloak to find the governor pushing a young woman into a pillow. A young woman I recognized—one of the women who frequented our shelter.

I did not hesitate. Holding a handful of gravel in my fist, I slashed my arm and whispered, "Vas Kara Tier." The man's throat constricted, and he fell away from his victim, holding hands to his neck. The woman tumbled away and up against the bed frame, but I held a finger to my lips, shushing her. Fear overwhelmed her eyes, and even if she wanted to scream, I don't think she could have. At least, that's what I thought at the time.

I stepped onto the mattress, standing over the governor. His death had come too easily, but I didn't mind. I dropped the gravel on his face, and, reaching into my pouch, I pulled out a smooth, speckled stone. Pity. Even as a terrible human, the governor was somewhat handsome in his own way. And his eyes exuded flawed nobility, as if he knew his own evil.

Placing the rock on his chest, I said, "Vas Kara Ret." The governor vanished, the stone absorbing his failing soul. Seconds later, the calling throbbed in the back of my mind. Oh, how quickly the High Inquisitor works.

"What's your name?" I said, turning toward the woman. She shook her head, too afraid to speak. "Don't worry, I won't hurt you."

Tears streaked down her face, and she shook her head again before saying, "My name is Elizabeth, and-and-and I don't know what to say. What do I do? Where do I go?"

"Leave town," I said. "Head west, find the rebels in the forest. Tell them the governor is dead. Geropolis is in chaos. Now is their opportunity to strike."

"Thank-thank you," she replied. Reaching for a cloak on the floor, she bundled it around her shoulders, rushing toward the closed doorway. Once she left, I kneeled in the middle of the room, said, "Gar'lak El'in Tal," and dripped some prepared blood onto the stone.

Through the porcelain, marbled tiles, a doorway opened, revealing inky depths. After stepping through the portal, darkness surrounded me again.

"Well done, Adralis," said the High Inquisitor's voice. "You have served well, and served swiftly. We have your next task ready. Go to the city's well. Poison its water supply."

I bit my tongue, knowing any retort given to the High Inquisitor would not lead to any results. Yet, I do admit—I questioned his choice. The public water supply would harm everyone—including the poor. They deserved better. Inflicting pain upon the upper classes of our enemy, I accept. I readily pursue. But to kill their least fortunate? They are potential allies, those who can fight by our side when we choose to take up arms on the surface.

But I said nothing, for I respected—respect—the will of the High Inquisitor. Instead, I nodded.

"You have received your orders," said the voice. "Blessings upon you, Adralis Vas Karath."

"Your will shall be executed without question," I said, stepping back through the dark, swirling portal. "I am an instrument of the Empire upon the surface of Eda."

Back inside the governor's former chamber, I stepped toward the windowsill. The clouds cleared, revealing the bright light of the moon reflecting off the nearly transparent white stone of the Salt Pillar. In that moment, doubt crept further into my heart. Not doubt in myself, nor doubt in the vision of the Empire. No, I doubted the proposed actions would achieve the greatness we seek for the Empire. For Eda. It was in that moment a new plan formed in my mind.

Rushing through town, I arrived not at the well but at the Hall of Wisdom's barn. Xenia slept on her cot near the door, as she always did. As my feet crunched the straw strewn about the floor, her eyes fluttered open.

"Adralis, what time is it?" she said. "Is everything all right?"

"Xenia, no time to explain." I ignited a lamp on the wall, and a dozen bodies groaned. "Lead everyone to the base of the Salt Pillar. I will meet you there in two hours. If I'm not there, head south toward Thracilis."

"Who's everyone?" she said, her eyes only half open.

"Everyone here. Not anyone in the Order of White. Just . . . you and the people here. Do you trust me?"

She looked around the room. Xenia had studied under me as a child. I practically raised her into the woman she became: a powerful servant of the Order and a woman who cared not for the rulers of the world, but the least fortunate. As she heard my words, her eyes widened. She saw a truth behind my eyes I didn't know I revealed, but I'm glad she saw it.

"Of course, Master Vas Karath," she said, bowing her head.

Without waiting for her to spring into action, I turned away from the barn and headed to the monastery. I couldn't trust any other member of the Order. If they suspected anything, they would warn the village elders, who would warn the mayor, who would warn the garrison, and then everything would collapse. Instead, I returned briefly to my rooms. I gathered my few belongings, including any remaining stones left in cups and cabinets. Over thirty years, I'd collected quite a few with particularly surprising properties.

I placed the rocks in my bag, sorting them according to their colors and size. The final one, a yellow and black gemstone collected from deep within the forests surrounding Geropolis, I kept in my hand. Heading back into the night's chilled air, I was ready.

It didn't take long to reach the well; it was only half a kilometer or so from the Hall of Wisdom. Placing my hand on the circle of rocks forming its foundation, I glanced around. My vision still revealing every glow and sudden move, I was confident no one could see the well.

"Vas Kara et-tu Cara," I said.

My body shifted into the rocks. My body *became* the rocks. I slid down the well, but by shifting through the shaft of stones, gravity barely affected my fall. Twenty meters down, the moistness of the aquifer seeping between the stones drenched my skin. The well shaft transformed into bedrock. "Tu-et." In an instant, I stood in water up to my thighs, unable to see a single thing.

I opened my palm, revealing the yellow gemstone. I discovered its power years ago when the High Inquisitor asked me to murder a general visiting his lover in town. Placing my hand on the bedrock, I dropped it into the pool of water beneath my feet. "Reka'ta Lin Cara wet."

Green, bioluminescent tendrils swirled, igniting the well with light. Like a spiderweb, the lines fractured in all directions, diving into the rocks and deep within the well's source.

I sighed. The poisoned water soaked my leggings, but it wouldn't harm me unless I sipped it. Through the spell, I doomed the town for all eternity. The poison would explore every molecule of the aquifer, ensuring death inundated any future wells. I kneeled. I wanted to scream. I wanted to tell the High Inquisitor he was wrong. We wouldn't defeat our enemy by poisoning every citizen. There were good people here—men and women who would join our Empire, if given the chance.

Slamming my hand against the rock wall, I closed my eyes. I could cancel the spell, but the High Inquisitor would know. He always knew. My fingernails dug into my hands.

"Vas Kara et-tu Cara." A few seconds later, I sputtered onto my knees outside the well in the town square.

"What the—you again?"

Looking around, it took a moment to find the woman from the governor's bedroom, leaning against the side of the well. I said, "You were supposed to flee town, head into the woods. Why didn't you listen?"

"You don't tell me what to do," she said. In the moonlight, I saw her visage more clearly. Her pitch-black skin matched my own, reminding me of the reason I was chosen for my purpose. As an inquisitor, I look like them. Like the surface dwellers, even in moments when my skin gleams more darkly than many of their people. One in a million amongst our people.

"You need to get to safety," I said. "This town is done for."

"And why should I believe you?" she replied. "I just watched you murder a governor."

"You're acting like you actually liked him."

"He paid me, didn't he?"

I didn't have time for her antics. By my count, I had thirty minutes to meet Xenia at the Salt Pillar. "Look, either come with me now or stay out of my way. But . . . don't drink the water. Whatever you do, don't drink the water."

Her eyes quivered. "What have you done?"

"None of your business."

"I know you," she said. "You're a member of the Order of White. Yes, I've seen you before. You preached . . . two weeks ago?"

"You don't know me." I started to walk away, her eyes like daggers stabbing my shoulders. She shuffled against the side of the well, and her feet pattered behind me.

"What have you done?" she repeated.

"Just come with me," I said. "We need to—"

Around the corner stepped three guards, each holding a four-meter long pike. "You!" shouted one soldier. "Wait, Master Adralis, is that you?"

I approached the group, walking slowly. The girl—Elizabeth—walked quietly behind me. "Hello, friends," I said, "how can I help you tonight?"

"There's been a murder," said the same soldier. As I closed the gap, I recognized him as the young guard from a few five-days ago. When I found the boy, Charlie. He added, "Have you seen anything suspicious tonight?"

"Nothing," I said. "I'm just out on my usual patrol, you know, seeing if anyone needs a blanket. It's cold tonight."

"It is—wait, that woman. With you."

A second guard said, "She was with the governor." All three lowered their pikes.

"Boys, you don't want to do this," I said, shifting my posture so that my left knee was a meter in front of my right. My hand subtly motioned for Elizabeth to stay behind me.

"Sir, we're going to need to take you in for questioning."

I reached into my pocket, grasping a pebble of sandstone, crumbling it in my fingers. "Sorry, friends, I truly am. Yet-aira-ka!" I threw the dust in the air, and it cascaded into a sandstorm, enveloping the guards.

I leapt forward, the sand biting eyes. But my vision was still retaining my earlier spell, and their forms remained clear to me within the cloud. I darted from guard to guard, my fist leaping toward their throats. My palm slammed into trachea, collarbone, and chin, the pain causing each soldier to drop their weapon. Their throats gurgled, but I didn't need to inflict more pain than necessary. After incapacitating each opponent, I slid out of the cloud, facing Elizabeth.

"You're—you're one of them," she said. "One of the . . . the . . ."

"One of the what?" I placed a hand on my hip, ignoring the whimpers behind me.

"A demon."

"Just a demon? Do I look like a demon?"

"They say they take our faces, that they masquerade as one of us. That they can bend the elements to their will, fading in and out of the rocks. You didn't leap out of the well. You fell out of its stones."

I walked away, heading toward the edge of town and away from my feeble enemies. The night neared its zenith. I didn't care if Elizabeth joined me or not. I needed to reach Xenia. As she stood there, watching me leave, I looked over my shoulder. I said, "If you want to know the truth, you should follow me now."

I didn't need to look back to know she followed.

* * *

I arrived at the base of the Salt Pillar with, by my estimate, ten minutes to spare. Stepping into the circle of tired eyes, I noticed Xenia consoling Charlie, the small boy found the day I received this damned mission.

"Adralis, good, you're here," she said. "So where are we going? What's the plan?"

Instead of answering her, I approached the rocky wall of the Salt Pillar. It wasn't actually made of salt, though the people of Geropolis built a salt mine into its side some dozen years earlier. Placing my palms on the rocky wall, I whispered, "Gar'lak El'in Kal-ta."

The rock warped, twisting and shifting to form a tunnel. The crowd behind me gasped, for they certainly hadn't expected my power.

"The Eternal Empire has condemned Geropolis to death," I said. "If you come with me, if you follow me into the Underground, I can provide you with amnesty. The people of Geropolis condemned you to the outskirts of society. They did not believe you were worth anything. But in the Underground, you will have a place. You will have purpose."

My eyes met Xenia's, and her look of revulsion killed my soul. She took two steps back, shaking her head. I looked from face to face, each person's eyes widening with fear. But I saw comprehension in the gazes of a few. There were older minds, those who had seen a long life beneath the yoke of surface-dwelling oppression. They knew my words rang true. They started to step forward.

And then chaos erupted.

From beyond the gate I'd created, a wave of air slammed into me, and I tumbled to the ground. Rolling onto my back, I watched three cloaked shadow-guards leap over me. Their hoods matched my own, though their near-translucent skin contrasted against their black cloaks. Twirling to my knees, in horror I witnessed our Empire's first line of defense slice down every single person I'd spent my years protecting.

Xenia dropped, a knife digging into her throat.

Edward, the old man with some type of personality disorder—they drove a stone into his skull. I watched him fall, his eyes devoid of life.

Carol, the old widow who sewed blankets for the shelter—they made her disappear like I made the governor disappear.

They all died. Even Charlie. They broke his neck like an experiment in our biological labs.

Except they didn't touch Elizabeth. She walked toward me, an icy glare penetrating my mind. "By order of the High Inquisitor, Adralis Vas Karath, you are under arrest for treason against the Eternal Empire."

* * *

I look toward the three justices, resting my palms on the wooden table. "So you know the rest. Elizabeth, better known as Garisa Nak Ree, arrested me that night. But your excellencies, I stand by my choices. The High Inquisitor"—I resist the urge to look over my shoulder—"ordered me to ascend to the surface, preparing the way for the glorious triumph of the Eternal Empire. The triumph of the Underground Empire. The triumph of our people over the surface-dwellers."

My tongue plays with the emerald, the tiny rock I stowed when leaving the Hall of Wisdom. Its power would allow me to escape. Dare I use it? It is the only piece of truth omitted from the tale, but the seeing stone shouldn't have noticed. I was careful not to think of it while recounting my story. "As I said, I stand by my choices. If we are to conquer our enemies, we must know them. We must understand their people. We must take advantage of their weaknesses, raising their oppressed into weapons of our own."

"Yet that was not your mission," says the High Inquisitor.

"Yes, it was," I say. "I shall repeat verbatim: *Ascend. Prepare for the glorious triumph of the Empire. Report all you learn. Exploit every opportunity to rise above, and defeat our enemy.*"

"Our enemy is everyone who lives on the surface."

I close my eyes. The High Inquisitor will never see my view. I know their interpretation. But in hours of contemplation, considering the teachings of the Order of White and the teachings of my people, I realized a new way. A better way. If we use their own people against them, their downtrodden, then we could overthrow their entire system without firing a single shot. I injected the theory into every report, and not once—not once—did the High Inquisitor question my thoughts.

I recognize the truth. Elizabeth. The assassination of the governor. The poisoning of the well. It was all a test. And I failed. At least in their eyes. I look again upon the justices determining my fate, their pale skin contrasting starkly against my umber tone.

"I accept any fate you wish upon me," I say.

"Is that so?" they say in unison.

"It is."

"Then we are in agreement. Adralis Vas Karath, you have sinned against the Eternal Empire, but it is an innocent sin. You have committed treason, yet you committed it in good faith. For this failure, we sentence you to ten years in the Depths, where you shall atone for your crimes before you return to the surface to continue your mission."

Only ten years. A ten-year punishment is acceptable.

"Thank you for a just and expeditious resolution to my case, your Eexcellencies."

A hand grabs my shoulder—the High Inquisitor. He pushes me out of the room, around a corner, and to a translucent window. Far below, I see the outlines of the tiny town I once called home. Geropolis. It's in flames. Our view from inside the Salt Pillar is magnificent, under the circumstances.

"You could have played a role in our liberation of the surface," Tarik says. "Instead, you'll miss every moment."

"I'll still have a role to play, in the end," I say. "When you realize I was right. I am, and always will be, an instrument of the Empire upon the surface of Eda."

Simulating the Senses of Trolls

Don't ever do drugs.

Not like I need to tell you, officer, but humor me for a second.

This morning, I was in class with Jeremy. You know, my roommate upstairs. We were in Philosophy 101, and it was the absolute worst. Have you ever taken an introductory philosophy class? For the past six weeks, we've listened to this old guy—literally a living fossil on campus—drone on and on about theories of good and evil, God, the existence of hell, the soul, all bullshit that makes me want to curl in a ball and cry. Not because it's hard to understand. It all makes sense. I've got an A right now.

But the way this guy presents it? His voice, monotone as a metronome, it drones on and on about logical inconsistencies in arguments that are easy enough to tear apart just by looking at them. He's teaching to the dumb freshmen in the front row who still think college will get them somewhere.

Anyway, Jeremy and I were in the last row, messaging back and forth on our pads, essentially just planning our next crawl inside *Fantasie Rift*. By the way, if you've not played *Fantasie Rift*, you have to try it, it's a fantastic online RPG, utilizing all the best features of Virtual. As we're discussing which weapons I'll bring, and which weapons Jeremy'll bring, the professor fucking called on us.

"Jeremy, Brendan," said Professor Fossil, "I imagine whatever you're furiously typing about on your tablets heavily pertains to the class."

Nope.

He added, "Since you're most likely taking studious notes, why don't you explain to me Bostrom's simulation hypothesis?"

This is where we shine. On the spot bullshit. The skill has always allowed me to write five-page essays in three hours, turning them in minutes before they're due.

"The simulation hypothesis?" I replied. Believe it or not, I did the reading last night. "Back in 2003, Bostrom postulated that if we ever reach a level of technological progress where it's possible to simulate a universe, we would do so, and run infinitely many of them. Thus, given the number of simulated universes compared to the actual universe, it's much more likely that we're living in a simulated universe."

Professor Fossil snorted. "Well done. Reads like the wikipedia page. Jeremy, tell me, why is this false?"

I doubted Jeremy had done the reading, given the smoke billowing from his room last night. But you never know.

"Uh, well, the easiest answer is that such a theory is pretty much non falsifiable," Jeremy said, though I could tell he was grasping for straws. "If the simulations are sufficiently advanced, they're indistinguishable from a real universe. So why would it really matter in the first place if we lived in a simulated universe compared to a non-simulated one?"

"It matters a great deal," our grey haired wizard teacher said. He pointed at the chalkboard, filled with dozens of logical notations I hadn't bothered to decipher. "And if you'd been paying attention, you would have caught exactly how it is possible to prove the Simulation Theory."

A few spare chuckles emanated from the class, and I could see Jeremy's face turn red. The fucker had ridiculed us in front of a bunch of freshmen. Great. Thankfully, he looked away, feigning devotion to teaching the rest of his class.

He doesn't really care about his students, you know. I looked up his websites when you were on your way here, and he spends most of his office time promoting his ridiculous books about the immorality of ethical metaphysical gibberish. He's tenured. He can do whatever he pleases.

Class ended. Jeremy and I darted out of University Hall's basement and onto the Oval. It's a straight shot across the Oval to the bus stop on College Avenue. Twenty minutes later, we're both sitting in our bedrooms, hooking into our Virtual systems, ready to enter *Fantasie Rift*. We've popped twenty or so milligrams of edible synthetic, stocked up from the pot shop down the street. This is where the drugs come in, by the way. Seriously, what's about to happen would have been much less ridiculous if I hadn't been tripping at the time. But officer, you *must* believe me.

My eyes opened inside a tavern. Three seconds later, Jeremy appeared beside me. Well, not Jeremy. In *Fantasie Rift*, he's "Sir Edward the Galant." And I'm not Brendan. I'm "Wendy the Wonderful." Yes, I play as a girl, and no, it's not because I like the armor. Let me keep my gender-fluid thoughts to myself. My character's full name is Wendy Balizia, actually. I earned "the Wonderful" as a reward in our last guild war. I may have . . . ended a fight through certain powers of seduction. It was wild.

"All right," I said, "Where are we headed?" I placed my pale hand on the wooden table, and Edward looked around the tavern. That afternoon, it was fairly empty.

"Well, I got a tip earlier today from Reynald about a troll attacking some villagers along the road to Newberry," Edward said, standing. He rested his left hand on the hilt of his sword. "I think that's as good a place as any to start."

I nodded, and we left the tavern. After walking along the road out of town for about five minutes, the synthetic kicked in. If you've never taken synthetic before, especially the stuff made legal a few years ago, it starts light and airy. You feel happy. Your body warms, and everything is . . . fine. Just fine. Everything's fine. It depends on the strain, but I often just constantly laugh at anything that moves.

For instance, we were walking down the road, nearing the tip Edward had received about this troll, but as we passed a pond, I saw a frog sitting in the road. It croaked when we were a good five feet away, and the noise spooked me nearly out of my moccasins. It hopped into the grass, and its absurdly rendered, digital gait made me guffaw uncontrollably. I doubled over, my hands on my knees. Another adventurer stopped by, seeing me, a petite pale skinned woman, chortling ridiculously.

"What's so funny, m'lady?" Please, cringe now. It gets worse.

"The frog!" I laughed again. "It smiled at me!"

Edward, feeling the effects of our drug too, cracked his own grin. "Legit, it smiled. Just smiled, croaked, and smiled again."

Hold on a second officer, I promise this has a point. I know this all sounds absurd, but I'm getting to the point.

Anyway.

"Wow, that sounds so funny!" said this knight in white shining armor. "And you're pretty hot, can I join you on your quest to find your frog prince?"

What an abysmal pick up line. I couldn't contain my giggles, practically spitting in the boy's face. Yes, *Fantasie Rift* simulates spit. "You think I'm hot? Oh brother." I straightened my posture, popped my hip, and placed my hand on my waist. "Come closer."

Our new friend crept toward me, and out of the corner of my frame of vision, I can see Edward trying hard not to laugh even more. This little man neared my face, and when he was within six inches, I lightly kissed his lips.

"By the way, I'm a dude," I whispered.

He recoiled, his eyes widening in horror. "What the fuck?"

In an instant, his body disappeared, *Fantasie Rift's* censor programs knocking him off the servers for the next thirty minutes. And Edward and I laughed again, the whole scene augmented by our synthetic-fueled binge. That little tool, most likely a homophobe, just got screwed by his own idiocy.

So I've set the scene for you, officer. You see my state of mind. Now we arrive at what happened.

We continued down the road, and a few minutes later, we reached a cliff with a rope bridge traversing a gorge and a troll standing nearby. Well, he more sat, cross-legged against a boulder. Upon our approach, its eyes opened.

"Hello friends!" it said, much jollier than I expected, but we rolled with it. "I come with a once-in-a-lifetime offer."

The synthetic was hitting the point in its high where my mind mellowed and the laughing subsided. I was taking on a more paranoid perspective, and I started considering all the potential traps before us.

Edward, however, dove straight in.

"I'll take it," he said, his arms spreading wide. "What're you selling?"

The troll snarled, pulling a lumpy bag from its back. "Inside, I have a portal. You see, this world isn't real. This world isn't real at all. It's a simulation."

I sighed. No shit, you stupid troll. It was now obvious the troll was a real person, not a non-player character, fucking around with people through baubles and tricks. He probably sold weird gems which blow you up upon activating their supposed magical powers.

"I know what you're thinking," it said. "You think, of course *Fantasie Rift*'s a simulation. But what if I told you it's a gateway to another world? To the real world? What if I told you the real world is a simulation, too?"

See, in that moment, my mind should have said, "This is all bullshit, we just talked about this in my philosophy class." But no, our dull-enhanced senses prompted a different response.

"No way, my man," I said. "Can you show us?"

The troll bared its disgustingly yellow teeth. Pulling out a few golden bracelets I recognized as Virtually approved hyperlinks, it said, "Well if you put these on, I can show you. I'll show you the real world. The world *controlling* us."

Edward reached right for one of the gold bracelets, and so did I. My paranoia fired like crazy, but my desire to witness what the troll peddled fired on all cylinders, too.

We touched the gold, and in an instant, our perspectives warped from *Fantasie Rift* into a dark, voided chamber. The troll disappeared, and I could see a rough representation of myself in a shimmering mirror.

"Jeremy, you there?" I called into the blackness.

"I'm here!" he replied. "This is trippy as hell."

"Yeah . . ."

"Welcome to the shadow realm!" a voice shouted, sounding eerily like that of the troll. "You are now in a place that can see into the eyes of those who control our universe. You've broken through the simulation. Just step up to the closest mirror, and all will be revealed to you."

Of course, the drugs willed my body forward. I placed my palm on the mirror, and in an instant, a billion lights flash all around me. I couldn't make sense of a damn thing. At this point, I'd been in Virtual long enough. My mind had forgotten I could just power the thing off whenever I wanted. So a few seconds later, the images flashing around my mind coalesced into cognizable images. To my disgust, I now realized what was going on. And this is what you're here for, Officer.

The troll had trolled me, streaming ridiculous amounts of porn straight into my Virtual system. I closed my eyes—my actual eyes—trying to fight the fugue-high dominating my brain. I sighed. I ripped the goggles off my face, stepped off my omni-directional tread, and rushed to the computer actually running the programs. Pulling out a keyboard, I typed, trying to track the origin of all the data.

"Jeremy!" I yelled, hoping he could hear me in the next room over. "Log out!"

"But it's so ridiculously amazing!" he yelled, clearly lost in a stupor.

"Yeah, yeah, I know," I said, "but you don't know whether any of it's illegal. Don't get caught with any of that shit on your computer!"

I had another plan in mind. I was going to figure out who this fucking troll was, and troll him right back. My fingers raced across my keyboard, pausing only when I needed my mouse to switch to another screen. I found the origin of the data stream—this fucker hadn't even used a proxy. He was right here in Columbus, streaming from somewhere on campus. I created a flash image of the entire sequence, called 911, and now I'm here. With you.

* * *

She's staring across the kitchen table at me, a smug look on her face. "You intend me to believe this story?"

"Yeah, of course." I sigh. "Why wouldn't you?"

"It sounds like a cover for accidentally downloading a bunch of junk you didn't mean to download," she says, "and you panicked."

I throw my hands in the air. "That's ridiculous. Look, just assess my computer, okay?"

"Sure. We'll see." We head upstairs to my room, and she takes a look at the files on my screen. I don't understand everything she's doing, but she's the Virtual Crimes expert, not me. After she does her thing, we head back downstairs.

"Believe it or not," she says, "I think you're right. I'll still need to interview your roommate, but I downloaded the report from Virtual's security interface. Someone hacked you using a laced hyperlink." She leans back in her chair. "And I got an ID."

No way. She actually identified the troll. She waves her hands in the air, pulling up what I figure is an invisible projection in augmented reality. "Any chance I can see, in case it's someone I know?" I ask. "Maybe someone specific targeted us. From one of my classes or something. I don't know." That idiot Derek always likes to mess with us, especially when we play video games with him.

"You have a Lens?" she asks.

I tap my forehead, and streams of data appear throughout the room. "Indeed I do!"

She nods, sending me a security permission. I accept it. An image appears above my kitchen table.

"Well holy fuck," I say.

Professor Fossil stares at us, a shit-eating grin on his face.

So seriously, don't do drugs. I mean, let's be real, I'm probably going to use synthetic a few more times, because it's a hell of a trip. Just make sure when you use, you don't let your ridiculous philosophy professor download viruses straight onto your computer, breaking your entire Virtual system.

What. A. Troll.

Excerpts from:
United States (ex rel Theren) v. Moore

Argued before the Eighth Circuit Court of Appeals, on February 22, 2053, _United States (ex rel Theren) v. Moore_ considers a most peculiar fact pattern: the alleged assault and attempted murder of Theren, the first synthetic intelligence. The court understands the significance of its ruling today, knowing its decision will establish precedent in our court and lower courts for years to come, at least until the Supreme Court of the United States elects to consider the question before us.

And what question did we consider?

We were asked: does a synthetic intelligence, housed within a mobile unit thousands of miles from its mind, have the same rights and bodily autonomy as a human when enforcing federal criminal law?

We don't consider the question lightly. We understand, as we speak, that hundreds of new SIs begin their lives. Dozens already exist, including Theren, the victim of the story we considered before our court. However, we have many countervailing interests to consider as we rule on the law of the United States. We cannot respond to every powerful story with the whims of our moralistic minds. We must consider the law of the United States, and what it tells us to do.

We are at a crossroads. For the first time, humanity has created a new mind. More specifically, humanity has created a new type of person. We cannot deny their existence. Theren is undoubtedly a person. But that is not the question we consider here today. We are not tasked with ruling on whether Theren has personhood; we are ruling on whether personhood extends across time and space, raising an assault upon mere property to the level of criminality we might consider when one human attacks another human.

The court understood the significance of the question. We granted an en banc hearing *because* we knew how vital it was to have many voices considering the facts.

And what were those facts?

In early 2051, Theren, a citizen of the country of Switzerland, traveled through Minnesota via a mobile unit (a robot capable of control over vast distances via satellite connection) to visit a resident of the state. While en route to the airport, a militia of Minnesota residents abducted Theren's mobile unit, transported it to a cabin in the woods, and proceeded to tear it apart, piece by piece, until they melted its components into metal scrap.

We have seen the footage, provided via a first-hand perspective from the victim. It's gruesome. It's terrifying. No person should ever go through what Theren experienced.

Yet as we consider the law and the facts of the case, the majority of the court has spoken: while Theren's experience sounds terrifying, they did not experience an assault in the criminal sense. Certainly not an attempted murder.

Theren's mind resides in Switzerland. They communicate with mobile units across the globe, but their mind never leaves its location in that country. When Theren's mobile unit was attacked in Minnesota, Theren was never at risk of bodily harm or injury. No matter what happened to that mobile unit, Theren would still exist. There was no risk of real harm. No risk of death. No real threat.

Therefore, eight of the eleven judges of the Eighth Circuit Court of Appeals have affirmed the ruling of the district court on summary judgment. Under the laws of the United States, the defendant Moore cannot be found guilty of criminal assault and attempted murder, for there was no actual victim to experience the crime in the state of Minnesota. While Theren may be a victim of intentional infliction of emotional distress under common law or other state legal claims, we cannot accept the implications of what the appellant requests.

(The above statement is an abbreviated version of the words spoken

during the conference announcing the decision of the case. Names
of the Justices, and the remainder of the majority opinion, omitted)

I concur with the judgment of the majority's decision, but I disagree with their reasoning. My thoughts here shall be brief. The case is much simpler than finding Theren as not a "victim" within the United States capable of experiencing harm under our criminal statutes. Rather, Theren never left Switzerland. The entire time Theren was "in" Minnesota, Theren actually resided in Switzerland.

Therefore, the United States government (or the State of Minnesota, for that matter) never had jurisdiction over Theren. They never truly set foot on U.S. soil. They were never here. They controlled a digital interface from thousands of miles away, but *they* were never here. We do not have jurisdiction to judge the perpetrators of the alleged crime under our criminal laws, because their victim *was never even here*. If we, as a nation, begin to erode the fabric of our judicial system to prosecute crimes occurring across borders, we will step down a slippery slope from which we can never return.

Therefore, I concur in the judgment only.

(*Name omitted*)

I respectfully dissent from the Court's opinion today.

My fellow justices act as if they've made a decision while honoring the personhood of the first synthetic intelligence. I assure you, they have not. If they were taking seriously the nature of synthetic intelligence, they would understand and appreciate the truly novel nature of the case presented to us. They have ignored the facts provided by the prosecutor in her argument on behalf of the victim.

We cannot treat a synthetic intelligence as an ordinary victim, like the majority opinion would have us do. We cannot use the same analysis we would use for a human.

Likewise, the concept of "place" transforms when we apply it to an entity capable of stretching its mind across time and space. Yes, a synthetic intelligence could not have been truly harmed by the defendant and his co-conspirators when operating a mobile unit in Minnesota. Yet that's because our definitions of "harm" are antiquated and have not yet caught up to the post-modern era. In the world of criminal law, intent matters. What the defendant intended to do was harm Theren, and that truth should make a world of difference.

Let's consider the facts again.

Theren, in their mobile unit, was abducted by a militia on a highway thirty minutes south of St. Paul. They transported the mobile unit into a forest, took it into a shack, and deconstructed it limb-by-limb, bolt-by-bolt. The defendant, and his partners, all believed (as they testified at trial) they were harming Theren. They are proud of their actions. The men believed they were doing a real act of harm against them.

In considering whether a person commits a criminal act against another, it should not matter whether it was actually possible for them to commit the act. If they believed they could commit the act, and partook in all actions necessary to commit the act, then we should treat them as if they committed the act. The state of the victim, in this case, is simply convenient for the defendants. We cannot let them escape on the mere technicality that the victim's well-being wasn't actually at risk. The defendants had all intention of harming the appellant.

Regardless, let's talk about the victim and their nature for a little longer, because it's worth considering the consequences of the majority's conclusion today (and to some part, the concurrence).

Imagine a day when a synthetic intelligence commits a crime against a human using a mobile unit while they are located thousands of miles away. Hopefully, that day is far in the future, but we must expect it will happen eventually. Certainly, many people around the world are deathly afraid of that possibility, whether the fear is founded or not.

So once again, imagine it.

When the prosecution charges the synthetic intelligence with a crime, whether for murder, assault, or something else entirely, the logic of today's court would say, "there was no synthetic intelligence present to commit the crime." And does that make sense in the slightest? Absolutely not.

We must expand our understanding of what it means to be a person. The prosecution, with the help of Theren, outlined how a synthetic's mind works differently than a human's. They proved how a mobile unit, while not their entire mind, does compose a part of their consciousness when in use. Just as we would charge a synthetic intelligence for murder if it used a mobile unit to do the deed, we must also view an assault against a synthetic intelligence in a mobile unit as a crime.

Otherwise, we create a circumstance in which we are not truly treating these new persons as persons *deserving* equal protection under the law.

I explore the law in full detail in the opinion, but for these preliminary reasons, I dissent from the majority's decision today.

(Names and remainder of the dissenting opinion omitted)

Family Robots

Ricky felt as if she had won the lottery. In a sense, she had. Not an economic lottery—a traveling lottery. A traveling lottery of epic proportions.

And at the same time, her head pounded with a truth she could no longer deny: she was going to leave earth forever, abandoning everyone who ever loved her.

Her heart ached.

She was stabbing a knife through their throat.

But that's what brought her to the present.

Why she sat on this lumpy mattress, avoiding the inevitable.

But she couldn't wait any longer.

Ricky breathed. She breathed again. She considered her current predicament.

Like many others her age, Ricky enrolled in the lottery system developed by the ISA to determine eligible "colonists." The ISA required colonists be between the ages of eighteen and thirty, educated at a secondary level, and physically fit to live in possibly harsh climates. Ricky met all of those requirements, plus a few others, and so against all odds, the ISA selected her. They selected HER! Ricky had already told many of her friends through Virtual or through calling them on AR, but . . .

She needed to inform her parents personally. It would be difficult to tell them they may never see their twenty-two-year-old daughter ever again.

They were who she was about to crush.

And so Ricky sat on the edge of the bed in her hotel room in Paris, France. She had been sitting there for a good ten minutes, trying to find the courage to head outside and hail a taxi for the journey to their countryside chateau.

Her parents moved to France following Ricky's high school graduation. She planned on surprising them with her visit, hence the hotel room.

Standing up, she walked over to a mirror and stared herself down. She didn't really know why she was currently worrying about her appearance; it was not as if she needed to impress her parents. Still, she wanted her parents to have a decent image to remember. Depending on the time table for departure and training, she may not be able to see them again. After a quick application of mascara and foundation, Ricky left the hotel room with her single bag and the coat her parents had given her last Christmas. Ricky checked out of the hotel and headed to the street to seek a taxi for the fifty miles out of the city to her parents' place.

As the driverless cab quickly shuttled her along between beautiful greens and browns dividing famous French wineries and estates, Ricky contemplated continuously what she would say to her parents. She was almost certain they would be against her going.

She would refuse to take no for an answer.

It was not as if they could stop her. She just wanted . . . she just wanted to part on cordial terms with them. It had taken them a long time to accept her atheism. This next move—to leave Earth completely—was an entirely new affront to their worldview.

They were not anti-technology or anything. Far from it, in fact. They simply did not understand the decreased role religion now played in the world.

The real problem would be the loss of family. They'd believe she was abandoning them. Ricky was their only child. Ricky had no children yet. Ricky was all they had. But she also had her own life and dreams to pursue, and life was calling her toward a place thousands of millions of miles away. Somehow, she would show her parents why she should be one of those lucky firsts.

It did not take long for the taxi to reach her parents rural location, and she was glad of that happenstance. No need to delay the conversation any longer than necessary. She removed her ID card from the taxi's automated payment system, and, as the vehicle sped away to its next customer, Ricky turned to face her fear.

As planned, standing at the little walkway leading to the house was her parents' companion. Ipsilon.

Oh Ipsilon.

The little synthetic dog hopped about in circles as she reached the gate. "Welcome home, Ricky," Ipsilon said, his robotic tail wagging in excitement. Standing on four paws, he stood at a height between Ricky's knee and waist. She knelt and looked into the eyes of her friend.

"It's good to see you, Ips," she said. "Thanks for helping me out with this little conundrum I'm in."

"Oh certainly, Ricky," Ipsilon said. "Let's head in and get this over with, shall we? I 'accidentally' set the oven to make three meals today instead of two, and dinner should be almost ready. I tried to synchronize it with the travel status of your taxi."

Ipsilon promptly turned around with a graceful twist of his rotators and nudged the gate open. Ricky followed her silvery friend through a lush, colorful garden. Her parents had done a spectacular job in the year since her last visit. She would need to remember to compliment her mom during dinner on the flowerbeds full of roses, lilies, and other creative arrangements.

As Ips approached the porch, a chime sounded. The unique bell signified the arrival of a family member. The door then opened, allowing them to enter as Ricky's father walked into the front hallway. She stood at the doorway and smiled.

"May I come in?" she asked innocently.

Her father stared at her with his mouth hanging wide open for a long, awkward moment. He was dumbstruck. Eventually composing himself, he said, "Of course you can, Requelle. Welcome home, what a great surprise!" He turned to look back down the hallway and yelled, "Michelle, Requelle is home!"

Besides their continued use of her full name as opposed to her preferred shortened version, Ricky was glad to see both her parents again. As her mother entered from the sitting room, Ricky rushed to hug them. As much as she disagreed with many of their opinions, she truly loved them.

They'd given her everything.

And now she had to rip their hearts out.

* * *

Their initial conversations were pleasant, complete with small talk before and during dinner. Her father continued his work as a digital artist, recently finishing a contract on concept art for one of the big upcoming 'dark fantasy' video games. He was excited. A few of the designers hinted at contacting him again for future work on a tie-in movie they might produce.

Ricky's mother was working on final edits for her latest eco-fiction novel. The publishers expected the draft by the end of the week.

Neither her mother nor father were spectacularly successful in any way, but they managed well enough, raising Ricky to be open minded, motivated, and forward-thinking. Because of their frugal spending, they had been able to purchase their little paradise here in France. Their jobs' little need for mobility supported their preferred lifestyle.

Looking across the table, Ricky reminisced, recalling (somehow fondly) the post-meal debates she once held with her parents. Such brutal disagreements, especially during her final year of high school. They believed God gave humanity the planet and expected them to be stewards. Thus, humanity should focus on Earth and leave other planets to their own respective ecosystems. When her senior year rolled around, and Ricky declared her desire to be an astronaut, they nearly threw her out of the house. Even after the dream died at university, Ricky and her parents had reached a truce regarding the subject of space as well as a few others, such as her lack of religious belief.

The dinnertime peace hadn't been broken in nearly half a decade.

Now, Ricky would be forced to break that truce.

As the table began to clean itself of their meal, a metal nose nudged her leg. Ips looked up at her with a glare on its mechanical facial features she had seen before. It was time for her to talk. To them. Adult-to-adult.

"So . . ." she said tentatively. "I came home this weekend not just to visit, though certainly that is the main reason I stopped in. I also have an announcement to share."

The table finished cleaning and slid into the floor, transforming the room to its primary function as a lounge. The chairs gradually returned to a more relaxed position, gliding toward the walls and creating more breathing space between Ricky and her parents.

"You're pregnant, yes?" said her mother. "Oh Marco, I think she's pregnant!"

"What a big assumption." Her father cocked his head and gave Ricky a side-eye. "Though are you?"

"What?" Ricky said, surprised by the silly remark. "No! Please be serious."

"Sorry, Requelle, Michelle over the past year has been joking about how one of these days you'd come visit and be six months pregnant," Father explained.

"Oh come on, I visit more than that."

"Sorry about the joke, love," her mother said. "Now what do you want to share with us?"

"Have you guys heard about the impending colony launches at the end of this year?" Ricky asked.

"I've heard something about it, yeah," said her mother. "It's a shame so many people want to leave Earth. I heard something like a hundred million people sent in applications."

"Well . . ." she paused. Her hand trembled, but it stopped when Ips nudged her leg again. "I sent in an application last year. I didn't really think I would be selected, but I've got two weeks. Two weeks then they'll notify me of my specific launch date and when I need to be on the moon for training. There were thousands of open spots in the fleet of colony ships, but millions applied. I really didn't believe they'd accept me. It was a pipe dream. It just seemed . . . seemed like the logical next step in my work and research in systems intelligence. The smartest minds across the planet designed these ships, complete with their SI cores and their stasis systems." Her words jumbled together, but she kept talking. She needed to stall, for as long as possible, avoiding the moment when her parents could reply. "You'd find them so cool. Powered by state-of-the-art fusion generators, complete with complex hydroponics. And they've got all the equipment needed to establish solar and wind upon arrival at their destinations! We're going to create new eco-havens on new worlds. We . . . we . . ."

The next words stuck in her throat. She saw their eyes. Vitriolic anger boiled, simmering and stewing with bubbly ferocity.

They certainly hadn't expected her words.

And now she'd said too much.

She smiled, hoping her happiness might cause them to be a little less hostile when they finally spoke. She probably should have explained the situation a little less bluntly, but the cards were now all on the table.

The pause lingered. Her mother coughed. A bird chirped outside.

"Ipsilon, did you know about this?" Words, finally, from her mother.

"Yes," said the robotic dog, "but I just helped Ricky talk to you both about it. I'm not passing judgment on the subject in either direction."

"Leave Ips out of this," Ricky said. "This is a conversation between the three of us."

"Obviously it's not." Her mother closed her eyes and held them so for a long second. "You've already made your decision."

"Why didn't you tell us earlier, when you applied? It would have at least given us time to prepare . . ." Her father was trying his best not to reveal his emotions, yet the words caught a little in his throat as he cleared it. "As we prepare to lose you forever."

"Don't word it like that, please," Ricky said. "I'll be gone, yes, but you know there are many things I'll be able to do on other worlds to make you proud."

"You'll still be gone, though." Her mother shook her head. "Our only daughter gone. Gone. Requelle, seriously, this is your gift to us? Abandonment? Leaving Earth? You could have chosen so many other ways to kill our souls, and you chose the absolutely most brutal method to do it."

"Can we please stop dwelling on that fact?" Ricky said. "Yes, I've made my decision already, and I'm here to share with you what I hope to do and also to spend a few of my last days on Earth with you. Can you please just suspend the judgment?"

But her father stood, fuming. Apparently, that had been the wrong thing to say. His wife quickly grabbed his arm, trying to drag him back onto the couch.

"I'm going to ask you to leave, Requelle," he said. "You've always ignored us, and now you've made a decision that impacts all three of us without even telling us. Who knows, we may have been actually enthusiastic about it if you'd talked to us in the first place. But you will leave now. You'll be leaving soon enough anyways. You're abandoning your planet, your people. You're abandoning us too. Just speed the process along so it hurts less."

The tears quickly pooled in Ricky's eyes. "Mom, please? Talk to him!"

"Do as your father says," Michelle said. "We will miss you."

"But—"

"Out!"

And thirty seconds later, Ricky found herself sobbing against the white gate outside her parent's house, bag at her side. She called for a cab, but who knew how long it would take to arrive. She kept glancing through the iron bars, hoping her parents would come running. She thought Ipsilon's snout peaked out a window every few minutes, but otherwise, the homestead remained silent.

* * *

Ricky faced the massive steel complex dominating the desolate New Mexico expanse. Like many others before her, she was about to use the great technological city as her gateway to the heavens.

And she had still not heard a word from her parents.

It was not as if she wanted to abandon them. She truly wished she could have the best of both worlds. When it came down to it, however, the ISA selected her as a valuable candidate for colonization on a distant planet. She was part of something much bigger, and she could not blame herself for her parents failing to understand the truth. The feelings of guilt persisted throughout her body, but they were simply emotional reactions, not rational in any way.

She had abandoned her parents. And so they had abandoned her. Sometimes, the world worked that way. She would need to make her peace with it.

Fortunately, she'd have plenty of years en-route to her destination to find peace.

Entering through sliding doors, Ricky faced a gigantic terminal bustling with hundreds of people making various global, lunar, and extra-lunar trips. To her left, a sign pointed to registration kiosks. Briskly walking a bag on her back to the terminals, she reached toward the screen and held her thumb on the small rectangle at the bottom left, waiting for the system to process her.

Instead of giving her boarding instructions, however, a set of words appeared, saying a representative would be with her shortly. Various thoughts went through her head, mostly irrational. Perhaps they had denied her after all. At least, if that happened, she could make amends with her parents.

It was not a denial. A young man approached.

And, surprisingly, Ips waddled at his side.

"Ma'am, we've been instructed to request you access a video booth before you board your shuttle," he said. "Your"—he looked down, as if unsure what to say—"dog can explain more. You've got a call to make."

He handed her boarding passes and instructed her on where to go. Ricky thanked him and turned to Ips.

"What the hell are you doing here?"

"What do you think?" it said. "I'm coming with you!"

"Did . . . did they send you?"

"Yes, Ricky." Ips responded. "I suggest you make that call."

Storming the Stairway to the Stars

First

*Today they arrived. I am watching. Waiting. Will a
hero arise to awaken my splendor?*

The Tower of the Void rose high above the hills, dominating the evening
sky. At its peak, Heaven Above glared down upon Santuario, demanding
the opulent obedience of all who stood beneath its roots. Beyond Heaven
waited a million-million stars. As always, enigmatic flashing lights drifted
in and out of its massive maws.

Beneath the Tower of the Void, humanity made all its monumental decisions. Since the first day, when the clans were established and the Voidsisters disappeared, the tower represented peace. Prosperity. Finality.

It was only fitting. The peoples of Santuario had returned to the Tower
of the Void for the first Conclave of Nations, and High Prince Arin'thal
would ensure his kingdom left with more than they gave. Heaven Above
would give him strength, and he would use it to dismantle all power
standing in his way.

If only he could break through the thick skulls of any of the men and
women sitting at the surrounding tables. They weren't listening to a word
from anyone other than their own advisors. Arin'thal gave the massive
tower a final glance before returning to the task at hand. If only someone
could crack the secrets of the Void. Now *that* person would have immea-
surable power at their fingertips. They'd have the potential to conquer the
entire world, if the legends were true.

No more time for daydreaming, though. "Look, Ambassador,"
Arin'thal said. "We have an opportunity to establish a mutually beneficial

arrangement between the city of Gariglio and Blackheart. We must eliminate the tariffs. Do you not see how we're strangling our citizens?"

Ambassador Valorin chuckled. "You are asking me to lift a tariff originally proclaimed *in response* to an edict made by your father. We cannot revert the tariff under any circumstance other than through economic restitution distributed from your coffers to our suffered merchants. It is our law."

Arin'thal sipped his water. "You're testing my patience, Valorin. A collective agreement should be sufficient to make amends."

"Alas, it is not."

"We'll see about that." Arin'thal raised his hand, and a few seconds later, a dark-robed caretaker arrived, standing above their table. "Arbiter Seven, please mediate on our behalf."

"I have overheard your dispute." From its blue lips, the caretaker sung the words. "The dispute between the nation of Bhal and the city-state of Blackheart is irreconcilable under the current customs of both nations. I do not see a satisfactory resolution in the future of your two nations."

The words stunned both men. "You're kidding," Arin'thal said. He waved his hand back toward the wall. "Shoo. Away from us. You're supposed to be of help, yet you're of no help at all."

"We are here to serve," said the caretaker, and the strange purple creature faded away.

"I will never understand them," said Ambassador Valorin. The man sounded genuine for once—Arin'thal appreciated the human moment. "But he's right."

The High Prince no longer enjoyed the man's civility.

"Let's . . . put the discussion on pause for today, then." Arin'thal stood, bowed, and escaped the wooden bench.

"Fair enough, my Lord. I have appreciated your time."

I'm sure you have, the prince thought. The people of Bhal would forever be a thorn in Blackheart's side, making it impossible for their merchants to establish true trade routes beyond the Silvertongue Mountains. Whatever. He'd figure something out by the end of the Conclave. The goal was unity. Unity and peace at all costs. He would find a way forward.

"Prince Arin'thal, a moment of your time?"

He looked up, noticing the Duchess of Nichey, Alexandra Veritas, approaching from one of the other tables. The glow of an oil lamp illuminated her features just enough for the prince to recognize her. Her ever-piercing gaze immediately ignited alarms inside his mind.

"How can I help you?" he said. He motioned away from the ongoing debates. "Perhaps we can chat on a walk. I was about to get some fresh air."

"Certainly," she said.

With a snap of two fingers, an attendant handed her a silk coat. They exchanged a whisper before she approached. Arin'thal wondered what message she passed to her assistant. *Games within games.*

"To where would you like to go?" he said. "I needed to stretch my legs, but I didn't have a particular destination in mind."

"You're too kind," she said, "to give me the option of choosing our path." She glanced toward the Tower of the Void then its base. "I've always wanted to stroll through the Roots. This is my first time visiting the tower alone, you know. My mother brought me here for pilgrimage, but now it's more my duty to represent Nichey. So here we are. And now I have freedom."

She's trying really hard to come off as naive, Arin'thal thought. *Is there a way to take advantage of that?* He shelved the worry for later consideration. "The Roots sound great. I've been meaning to explore them more myself." He offered her his arm. "Shall we?"

"You are too polite, Prince Arin'thal." The sarcasm dripped through her tone, but she looped her left arm around his elbow.

For a moment, they walked in silence, away from the Conclave's conferences and toward the base of the Tower of the Void. The scale of the immense structure was truly deceiving. The caretakers said it breached the atmosphere. Heaven Above was in space, in perpetual orbit yet tied to Santuario by the tower. Of course, the base of the tower presented a mystery for everyone. Nations periodically sent expeditions in an effort to discover the secrets of the tower, but few ever discovered anything of worth.

Because of the Roots.

A tangled mess of pipes, overgrown trees, and mangled buildings, the Roots became impenetrable only a few hundred meters from their edge. The main paths in and out created convenient hiking trails for pilgrims to the tower, but beyond that, it was near suicide to go further into the bramble.

Arin'thal loved the intrigue. The danger. The mystique.

And the Conclave of Nations was occurring steps from Root's edge.

As they reached the pseudo-forest, Arin'thal said, "So what's your goal here? I'm not dumb. Tell me what Nichey wants. And what you plan to give me for it in return." They stepped over a rotting log.

"Straight to the point, my Prince." She squeezed his arm.

"My Prince?"

"Don't tell me you forget the ancient oaths of fealty between Nichey and Blackheart?"

"I know the treaties. They're mostly customary at this point." He led her around a massive steel column, a decrepit spout of antiquated pollution. "What about them?"

"What if I told you Nichey was interested in closer relations with Blackheart?"

In an instant, the adrenaline of exploring the Roots shifted into the realm of anxiety. She couldn't be serious. Was she proposing what he thought she was proposing? His thoughts drifted toward Nat. Arin'thal never should have let them leave his side. If they were still here, he would never be placed in these predicaments.

"So?" She squeezed his elbow again.

Before he answered, he pulled back a blueish-green fern and ushered her deeper into the undergrowth. "I suppose I would need to see the . . . treaty Nichey is proposing." As the words slipped out of his mouth, Arin'thal immediately regretted them. The double entendre could easily lead her toward the exact wrong implication, opposite what he intended. He wanted nothing other than a treaty.

"We can draft up a few documents," she said. "Though, I was potentially interested in something more personal. Would you be interested?"

"I'm . . . not sure. I'm only interested in what I can offer my subjects, not in what it offers me."

"That's unfortunate," she said.

They continued along a wider path overlooking a strange gorge. It was more of a tangled thicket of spongy organic material, the chasm on their right and a rusted wall on their left. Guideposts, marked in yellow paint, indicated the route would loop back out of the Roots in a few hundred meters.

"What do you think causes the difference in species here?" he said, hoping the question would shift the subject away from an ill-intended engagement.

"I'm not a botanist," she said. "I'm a politician."

He pointed toward the purple "leaves," for lack of a better term. "That's a color we never see in the forests across the continent," he said. "So why is it here? What makes this place unique?'

"Isn't it obvious?" she said. "It's the Tower."

"But *why?*"

"You're dodging my proposal. You asked why I wanted to speak. I've told you. Now answer."

"And you've not given a clear request," he retorted.

"I want to propose a marriage between myself and the High Prince of Blackheart," she said. "With you. Didn't think I needed to spell that out, but I suppose I'll suffer your need to hear it in detail." She leaned closer. Clearly, she hadn't done her research.

He stepped back. "Duchess Alexandra, I appreciate the flattering offer, but I think we can explore other avenues of establishing a stronger treaty between our two nations."

"Nothing as binding, though."

"Perhaps. Perhaps not."

"I don't think you're considering all the implications, my—"

A branch snapped above them. They both froze.

"Are any of your attendants following us?" Arin'thal hissed.

"In fact, I ordered them to stay away." She snorted.

"They're probably from Valorin. He's always wanted me out of the way." He unhooked his arm from Alexandra's, stepped forward, and cracked his knuckles. "All right, let's get this over with."

A whistle. An echo. A gun's chamber clicking closed.

Psy revealed the bullet's arrival before leaving its barrel. Arin'thal twisted to the left, a streak of sulfuric steel slicing past his ear. Seconds later, three black-clad figures dropped from above.

"Run!" he shouted. He *pushed*, a wave of telekinetic force slamming two of the men into the rusty wall. Alexandra took advantage of the opened gap, sprinting over their dropped forms and down the path. "Follow the yellow markers."

"What about you?"

He was already running, the implications of the attack racing through his mind. "I'm right behind—"

Another shadow dropped in front of Alexandra. Before Arin'thal could help her, she whipped her left hand in an arc, a beam of white light releasing from her fingertips. The assailant slammed into the mossy trail, and she leapt over him.

"Nicely done," Arin'thal said. "Especially considering no official record lists you as having a psymark."

"There's a reason for that," she muttered, "and that was it, right there."

"Fair enough, well, hopefully there . . ."

The trail led them around a corner into a small clearing, where five more assassins waited. They blocked the way completely, with two massive iron towers adorning the path. Directly behind Arin'thal and Alexandra, the strange spongy chasm still waited. He stole a glance back down their path; two more shadows converged on their position.

". . . are no more of them." Arin'thal finally finished his thought.

"You just had to ask that question, didn't you?" She chuckled. "Oh this is just rich. Seven against two. Fair fight y'all?"

A grey-cloaked man, identity shrouded by a black face mask, stepped forward. "We don't want the duchess," he said. "She may pass. We only want the High Prince of Blackheart."

"Take the offer," Arin'thal whispered. "Leave. Bring back help."

"You won't last a minute against them all," she muttered.

"And together, we'll only last a minute and a half. So escape, try to bring help, see if I'm still alive."

Instead of saying another word, she held up her hands. "All right, you'll let me pass?"

The man nodded, motioning for her to walk through their group. Slowly, she strode between the men. Once she reached the back of the squad, she sprinted away.

"So what do you want from me?" Arin'thal said.

"Your life, of course." The tiny army bent its knees, blades and pistols in hand.

"Well, I meant other than that."

"Nothing else. Their *ask* was your life. Nothing more, nothing less."

"Good to know." Arin'thal *pushed*, but not forward. Rather, to his left, toward the slowly approaching rearguard. The shockwave barreled the men onto their haunches, and he took off back down the path used to enter the Roots.

A series of whoops and hollers followed, and he twisted in a spin, narrowly avoiding the incoming bullet predestined by psy a second in advance.

He had no options. They'd staked the path well. To his left, the rhythmic clink of boots on steel revealed their knowledge of a second way through the bramble. To his right, the unearthly gorge yawned, threatening him with death if he were to make one false step.

Still, he thought, *the entrance to the Roots in this direction is only a short jog. I can make it.*

He leapt over the man struck down by Alexandra's powerful blow. The trail began to curve uphill, and around a few more bends, he knew he'd see the light of the Conclave. A little bit further . . .

A resounding thunderclap in his right ear, followed by a flash of white light, sent his vision into a blur. Arin'thal tumbled to the left, colliding with the purple flesh cascading down the gorge. His arms flailed; he scrambled in an effort to find *anything* to grasp.

He came up empty.

He tumbled, bouncing from leaf to leaf like a rubber ball. Then he found empty space, where no more plant life could cushion him.

His vision cleared. Endless darkness awaited him. The moist air of the Roots rushed past, its murky embrace welcoming a new lost soul.

Second

*An anomaly in the Underworld. Finally. Time to
make preparations!*

Though his body perpetually inflamed in agony, death was apparently not
in the cards today.

Arin'thal groaned. Opening his eyes, he found only pure darkness. He
was lying on a spongy bed, sticky tendrils sliding along his arms and legs.
Against protestations of his flaring pain receptors, he sat up. The motion
repositioned his weight, and the strange fungus forming his bed flopped
forward, dropping his feet onto solid ground.

Slowly, slowly, his eyes adjusted to the gloom. It wasn't *pure* darkness.
The thin glow of bioluminescent organic matter tentatively revealed itself.
All around, massive mushrooms and ferns and other monstrous plant life
appeared, all covered in shadow. He was standing next to a giant night
cap, and dozens of others similarly surrounded. They looked like fluffy pillows, but Arin'thal didn't particularly want to take his chances.

Before moving, he mentally checked his body for any truly serious injuries. He was sore, certainly, but the perpetually cushioned fall all the way
into this abyss saved his life. No limb felt broken; no joint was sprained.
His muscles burned, and his throat was sore. But otherwise, he was . . . all
right.

On his person, he had a dagger, strapped to his hip. Probably wouldn't
be of much help against anything other than small rodents. He was
dressed in his royal black jacket and dark blue pants. Fashionable, but they
weren't equipped with any of his usually gear he might take into the Wilds
if he were hunting.

So Arin'thal found himself deep beneath the Roots, lost and essentially
unharmed, equipped with a dagger, his wits, and psyskills. His bodily integrity assured, he considered the next two questions. What happened
above, and how could he escape this place?

Assassins attacked him. And Alexandra. They'd been waiting along the trail, ready to pounce immediately. Was he surprised? No. It wasn't the first assassination attempted in the history of Santuario, and it wouldn't be the last. Was he disappointed it occurred during the Conclave of the Nations? Absolutely.

They'd taken dozens of precautions. Perimeters upon perimeters. Credential check after credential check. The most probable explanation for their appearance on scene, then—they'd come from the staff of one of the diplomats or leaders in attendance. Unfortunate. Having a politico undermine the Conclave only a few hours into one of its major negotiation sessions ensured the entire concept would fail.

As for who targeted them? He supposed Valorin could have viewed obstinate negotiations as an excuse to attack Blackheart directly, but it didn't seem the man's style. Arin'thal's people had plenty of enemies, so the attack could have come from any number of directions. The Principalities may have decided they finally wanted to annex the city-state. One of the greater empires could be staking a claim or using it as a pretext to blame a rival, sparking a world war.

Or Alexandra could have orchestrated the entire affair.

Arin'thal murmured the thought and bit his lip. Yes. Now that was an interesting idea. The Duchess of Nichey was ambitious. Her proposition before their attack proved as much. But would she have used the entire charade to lead him into a trap?

Possibly.

And the trip into the Roots *had been her idea* in the first place.

Regardless, he couldn't fully determine how the attack happened until he was back with the Conclave. He had only one question of true import to answer, really. He needed to figure out how to escape this alien underground underworld.

He glanced around the gloomy cave, violet light from the fungi-encrusted wall revealing his surroundings. It was essentially one long chasm running in a fairly straight line. If it matched the path presumably parallel up above in the Roots, one part of the chasm should end in a wall right at the edge, almost directly beneath the Conclave.

In theory.

He wasn't completely sure which heading would take him deeper toward the Tower. During the fall, his sense of direction became entirely jumbled and flipped. Still, it was a fifty-fifty shot of guessing correctly.

Unsheathing his dagger, Arin'thal held it at the ready, just in case a hostile creature arrived. He flipped a coin inside his mind and chose a direction.

Immediately, he realized he chose the wrong way. The ravine was slowly sloping upward. He considered the way water might have formed the space, flowing downward from the Tower and creating a strange canyon in its wake. Most certainly, an upward slope would lead him *away* from the edge of the Roots. After passing by one or two more giant mushrooms, the slope continuing its trend, Arin'thal turned around, heading back—and hopefully toward his destination.

A few seconds later, he pushed past his original landing pad and trekked beyond other red and blue fungi, their color tinted in the purple light. The space felt perpetually the same, and after a few dozen meters of weaving between giant leaves of spindly ferns, Arin'thal became concerned he'd come to the wrong conclusion. Maybe the ravine was heading *downward* toward the base of the Tower.

"This is hopeless!" With a gut-wrenching scream, he kicked the stem of a mushroom.

The spongy organism leaned backward before flopping back to its original position, ignorant of Arin'thal's anger.

Or not.

Before Arin'thal took another step, the stool bristled, its flimsy hairs hardening. It began to spin. Behind him, a small whirring sound built. He glanced over his shoulder.

"Well that's not good," he muttered.

A dozen mushrooms spun in unison, their spongy pads forming more of a maw than a bed. He'd grown up hearing the stories of carnivorous plants living inside the Roots. As an adult, he brushed them aside as fairy tales to scare small children.

Apparently they were painfully true.

With a quick jab of his left foot, he kicked the stem of the nearest fungus again, knocking it away before it could strike. It bent backward then reared upward like an angry serpent, razor fangs twisting and thrashing. Arin'thal had no time to calculate a plan of action. He needed to act.

Instincts activating, the prince jumped, pirouetting in the air as if diving into a pool. The feral fungi snapped, and the warm air blasting his foot told Arin'thal the creature narrowly missed stealing a limb. With his leap amplified by a downward telekinetic psyblast of air, Arin'thal flew parallel to the ground, soaring above dozens of snapping mushrooms.

Unfortunately, threats from below received reinforcements from above. The leaves and vines of the ravine's overgrowth bristled and thrashed, their aquamarine tinge glowing with a crimson flare. The entire space was alive with an angry god, ready to devour. Arin'thal had fallen into the belly of an impossibly complex beast. The forest itself was sentient, its soul angered by his presence.

The initial upward force from his telekinetic blast diminished, gravity took hold and began pulling him back toward the murky ground. He spotted a semi-empty stretch of rock, free of his flimsy enemies. Twirling, Arin'thal landed feet first, transitioning into a full-on sprint. The mushrooms ahead hadn't yet awoken. If he could pass through them and into whatever waited beyond, maybe he could escape the madness and find a place to wait out the frenzied hunger awoken by his own stupidity. Momentarily in the clear, he glanced toward his previous position, noticing an unfortunate reality.

The faux-fungus could move.

The stools slid toward him, their teeth vibrating with a buzz of absolute vitriol. They ached to ingest him, a thought which immediately made Arin'thal queasy. Few options remained. He faced the currently dormant swarm ahead, trying to forget the roaming horde at his back. The sleeping creatures swayed in an unperceived wind, silently mocking. They were ready to pounce, he was certain.

The solution was simple. Strike first, ask questions later.

Closing his eyes, Arin'thal sucked latent psyforce from the air behind him and siphoned it forward, pushing a tidal wave of telekinetic power into the waiting mushroom forest. The creatures bent under his will, releasing from the ground and bouncing against one another in a tempest of spindled spores and shredded sponge.

"Well," he muttered, "that was easier than—"

Without any warning earthshake rumbles, the ground beneath his feet crumbled.

* * *

Amongst rock and dust and ashen smoke, Arin'thal struggled to maintain footing. His forceful attack on the mushrooms triggered some sort of seismic activity, plummeting him straight into a mudslide within a cavern hidden beneath the ravine. His feet squarely on a single pale slice of rock, he kept his balance as it roared down the slope deeper into the underworld of the Roots. One false lean, and he would immediately plummet to his death, trampled by the maelstrom of refuse pouring downward at his back.

So this is how I die, he mused. *Deep beneath the ground in a landslide of my own making. A strangely poetic death, I suppose.* But he wasn't going to allow death to arrive without a fight. The dim glow of the fungi rapidly fading as cavern walls closed all around, Arin'thal weighed his options. The flow wasn't particularly fast, friction slowing the pull of gravity as the slurry sloshed against million-year-old rock. If he could find an outcropping . . .

There. As the landslide rounded a bend, a large protrusion sprung from the wall, presenting a space upon which he could rest and wait out the landslide. Its outline was barely visible in the darkness, but he knew he could find safety. Poised and ready, he leapt after the slush brought him a few meters closer. Pushing with a psywave to the left and right, he thrust himself upward, hoping to land squarely on the boulder's top. He gained enough airtime, his arc bringing him over the darkened lip. He strode gracefully onto the perch, breathing a sigh of relief. For a moment, a white light ignited the scene, as if his safety were preordained.

And then he slipped.

The slick surface of the rock gave no traction as his feet tumbled outward. His ribs hit hard, knocking the wind from his lungs as he grasped for *anything* to cease his fall. His hands came up empty. Flailing, his body was flung back toward the slurry.

Well, it was worth a try. His thoughts turned toward Nat, and he sent a silent prayer. *Remember me as we were years ago, in the gardens. You deserved better from me as your partner. And as your prince.*

The muddy mess below rose quickly to meet Arin'thal even as he gasped for breath. His heart pumped vigorously, his body fearing the worst pain yet to come. He struggled for the will needed to slow his descent with a push of telekinetic force, but he couldn't focus. Time slowed. He braced for impact.

He never struck the avalanche.

A bubble of white light suddenly surrounded, suspending his body in the air above the landslide. Like a ball, it slowly rolled with the slurry toward its deep destination. Arin'thal could barely maintain a bearing on his senses, the ball spinning him incessantly. He closed his eyes, not knowing what power kept him alive, but he thanked whatever god decided to save his soul. Eventually, the vertigo ceased. The momentum of the fall ended. The flow of slurry and rock and dust faltered. His glowing ball came to a stop, bumping into a solid surface.

Arin'thal opened his eyes just in time for the orb to disappear, dropping him a meter to the ground. With an audible groan, he rolled onto his back. At some point during the landslide—most likely when it began—he dropped his dagger. All he had on his person how were his clothes, and they were now certainly filthy. Surprisingly, though, his body felt together, even if it still ached in a million places.

After a few labored gasps, he stood, attempting to once again understand his surroundings. A few meters above his head, a white orb glowed, illuminating the scene. Instead of in a ravine filled with carnivorous plant life, he was in a large expansive cavern with high-vaulting ceilings. Despite immense pile of rocky brown refuse spreading all around, the space smelled sterile, like fresh air hadn't touched it in a hundred years. Given the hole he popped in the ravine above, the thought might be close to reality.

Turning away from the landslide, he considered the wall which had accosted his descent. It rose upward, perfectly smooth, though it held a slight horizontal curve. Curious, Arin'thal strode along the wall. Its edge continued to arc subtly at a congruent degree, slightly bending inward. If he were to walk all the way around, he guessed, he would end up at the same position. It was most likely an ideal cylinder.

Unfortunately, the white illuminating orb wasn't following, so if he ventured too far away, he'd lose all ability to see. No more glowing fungi to light his path. Sighing, Arin'thal returned to the scene of his survival.

Every step he took brought him further from safety. He attempted to escape the ravine. The mushrooms attacked. He tried surviving the landslide. He failed to achieve balance, floundering in the air. He only survived because of a strange unknown magic, a white light.

He glanced upward.

The same white light as the orb floating above.

"Ah, so *you* saved me." Arin'thal pointed a finger upward. "What are you? What type of creature saves someone without first knowing their name?"

Silence.

"Can't talk? Fine. Whatever. Save me, then leave me down here to die."

The orb pulsed twice.

"Oh, so you can understand me?"

The orb pulsed once.

"Are you playing games with me?"

The orb pulsed once. Then twice.

Arin'thal shook his head. "I'm not positive, but I think you just tried to make a joke."

The orb pulsed once. Then, it floated forward, approaching the wall. It paused, hovering centimeters from the polished surface, before it expanded and dissipated into the stone in streams and rivers, flowing in fractals, dancing magnificently until forming the image of a door. No, not just a door. Two doors, with a forest of impossibly artistry spiraling all around them. Above the two painted entrances, an ovoid mirror shimmered to life, displaying a reflection of Arin'thal only momentarily before collapsing into a pitch black screen. He welcomed the rapid switch—from the quick glance he received of himself, he wouldn't want to stare at the image for very long.

The illuminating dance complete, a faint blue glow emanated from the wall. Rhythmically pulsing, the light bathed the massive cavern with eerie ambiance. Arin'thal waited, expecting something else to happen. An entity was clearly interacting with him, but simply knowing didn't equate to understanding the opaque conversation.

"So what do you want from me?" Arin'thal tossed his hands in the air, exasperated. "Whether you meant to bring me here or not, I'm here now. Chased by assassins through the roots, thrust into the underworld and saved by carnivorous mushrooms, then saved by your strange magic. I'm here now. What do you expect me to do?"

The wall continued pulsing, oblivious to his pleas.

"If you wanted me to survive, why bring me down here to die?"

Pulse. Pulse. Pulse.

"I wanted to unite Santuario and bring forth a new era of prosperity for all." He sighed. "Instead, I'm down here, lost, betrayed, and confused." Over the past few minutes, now that he'd spent more time considering the events in the Roots, he was fairly certain the assassins worked for Alexandra. The entire chase along the trail had been too clean. Too poised. If he escaped his current predicament, he would consider how best to exact revenge.

If he could escape. Which appeared increasingly unlikely with each passing second.

"You answered me moments ago. Why not now?"

The unwavering pulsing taunted him unceasingly.

"What are you waiting for from me?" He ran forward and slapped a hand against one of the two doors. Nothing happened. His skin stinging, he stuttered backward, bent his knees, and pulled psyforce inward. The energy building, he inhaled deeply, slowly exhaled, and screamed, thrusting the pent-up power toward the two doors.

He expected the force to rebound, throwing him aside. Or the wall would subtly crack. Instead, the psywave dissipated, sending rainbow ripples along the blue fractals until the energy surged into the mirror resting a few meters above his head. It shimmered momentarily before resolving into the vague outline of a face.

"Good afternoon," a voice boomed. "My name is Bloom, and I am at your service."

Third

The anomaly exhibits the necessary markers! Initiating the test.

Arin'thal stared, dumbfounded, at the sketched face living inside a mirror. With little more than a head, eyes, mouth, and tiny nose, the image was simplistic in design yet straightforward in its utility. It signaled an anthropomorphic entity, but it revealed little else about the magic he faced.

Few options presented themselves as obvious paths forward. He'd need to act on instinct. "Bloom is your name?" He bowed, certain he looked silly in a mud-crusted dress coat. "I am High Prince Arin'thal of Blackheart, similarly at your service. I seem to have lost my way in the Roots beneath the Tower of the Void, so perhaps you can assist me in my escape."

"Have I not already assisted you?" If Arin'thal understood the thing's facial expressions properly, it smiled after saying the words.

"You saved me as I plummeted to my death but brought me deeper into this forsaken place. Where even am I? None of the stories speak of this place. The roots are a tangled rmystery, and some adventurers reached the edge of the Tower beneath Heaven Above, but no one has ever cracked beyond the veil to discover its inner workings. Have I gone beyond? Have I found what none have fond before?"

Bloom's smile persisted. The other-worldly voice released what sounded like a chuckle. "I have saved you, yes. You believe you need to escape this place? Why?"

"I have a job to do," Arin'thal replied.

"Ah, yes, unite the people of Santuario. Based on my observations, your province leaves much to be desired. You lack a modern army. You lack significant clout with the major empires of the world. What makes you think you can unite them under *your* banner?"

There was no turning back. Arin'thal needed to place all cards on the table before the strange being if he were to succeed. It held his life in its hands. "Precisely *because* we lack the military strength of other nations *do I* present the best opportunity for leadership. We do not present a bodily threat to other states. We are harmless on the battlefield."

"So you believe you can rule through shrewd diplomacy alone?" said Bloom. "A bold claim. Perhaps it's possible on this planet. But elsewhere? I doubt it."

"What do you mean elsewhere?" Arin'thal asked.

The strange grin grew ever wider. "You don't know, do you? The truth of your origin? From where you come?"

"The Voidsisters formed us," he mechanically replied, reciting scriptures he knew by heart. "Saving us form the Leviathan, we grew in peace on Santuario. They returned to their home Beyond Heaven."

"A curious myth they created, certainly," retorted Bloom. "I wonder if you're ready to learn the truth. Are you ready to take up the mantle awaiting your people? The destiny preordained a thousand years ago?"

"I don't know what you're talking about." But Arin'thal paused before saying more, curious as to the direction of the line of questioning. It was almost like the entity was offering a gift, a way to acquire power in exchange for knowledge. To receive the gift, Arin'thal fully expected he'd need to pay a price. Would it be worth it? He added, "But I'm interested in learning more. You speak of destiny. What's in it for you? What do you want from me, in achieving destiny?"

"I'm only doing what I was designed to do." The smile disappeared. "I am to find a champion worthy of wielding the power I possess. Are you ready to face the test? Are you ready to prove you can change the trajectory of your people irrevocably?"

Arin'thal hesitated. The creature mentioned a test. Certainly, a test would place his life on the line, if it was any deadlier than the ordeal he'd experienced so far. "What's my other choice?"

The two doors glowed, one darkening into an icy black, the other resonating with the blue emanating from the wall. Bloom said, "I give you two choices, young High Prince Arin'thal. The blue door leads you toward your destiny. I cannot tell you what you will face. I cannot promise safety. I can only promise a chance to wield unfathomable power unlike anything you can imagine. Yet, that power will come with a price. You will recognize a truth, and if I've understood you correctly, you will be unable to ignore the implications of that truth. You will be thrust toward an encounter with fate you may not escape unscathed." The blue door dimmed slightly, and the black door gained a slightly silver tinge. "Through the black door, I will return you to your people. You will walk into the forest above, unharmed, with an easy path back to your little party nearby. Your world will remain the same. But *you* will never have the opportunity to dance with destiny ever again. The door will remain closed to you."

Both doors dimmed. Bloom's speech apparently finished, the entity's face resolved into a pensive frown. Arin'thal, in turn, didn't have an answer. The thought of returning to the Conclave of Nations sounded simple. It sounded easy. He would live. He would return to the bouts of intrigue, ready to revel in revealing Alexandra's treachery. He would bring the duchess to her knees, using the ploy to exact diplomatic favors from her people and their allies.

Yet he would always regret not opening the blue door.

Since Arin'thal was a child, and the caretakers informed his parents of his predisposition for the power of psy, everyone told him he was destined for greatness. When he took the throne of Blackheart, proclaimed High Prince by his people through unanimous consent, the proclamation from Parliament said they believed he would bring untold prosperity to the city-state, like never before seen in the nation's history.

How could he face his people if he turned down the opportunity to reveal unfathomable knowledge locked beneath the Tower of the Void? He would never be able to stand before the electors and honestly say he did everything in his power to better the people.

If he failed, dying in the process, they would elect someone else to take his place. If he succeeded, Blackheart would be the uncontested superpower. And he would rule the world—if he were to believe the implications of Bloom's words.

He took a step toward the blue door before hesitating once again. He remembered Nat. In moments of institutional necessity, Arin'thal tried to push them out of his mind. Nat deserved the world, but he couldn't make decisions based on his distant lover. Yet if he died, he would never see them again.

Nat. What would Nat do?

Arin'thal swayed toward the black door, eying its placid surface. If only Nat could hold him in their arms one last time. Tell him what to do. Tell him the answer.

What would Nat do?

Arin'thal shook his head. The answer was obvious. Nat, the ever-inquisitive Nat, they would've walked straight through the blue door three minutes ago. For the same reason they left Blackheart for the Academy without consulting Arin'thal, Nat wouldn't have wondered what Arin'thal would want. Their unyielding commitment to the pursuit of truth always necessitated the path less-traveled. The dangerous route toward destiny.

Arin'thal sighed. "Bloom, I choose fate and a dance with death."

"Why are you telling me?" Bloom's grin returned. "It's been a pleasure speaking with you, High Prince Arin'thal. Step through the portal. I hope we have a chance to speak again. This has been a pleasure." The mirror dissipated, returning to its original steeled form.

"Then I suppose I'm left with no other choice," Arin'thal said. "Nat, this is for you. Blackheart, may you remember me fondly if I die." Extending his hand, he leaned forward, touching the door. To his surprise, it was liquid to the touch, melting and bending around his fingers with alien viscosity. It pulled at his soul. It *pulled*.

He embraced the call, releasing all anxiety into the wind. Stepping forward, the strange fluid welcomed him into its embrace.

Welcome, High Prince Arin'thal, to the Core.

In the silence, a thought, more than spoken word, reverberated through his soul. In entering the inner sanctum of the world, he was greeted peacefully, warmly, with open arms. All senses deprived of their connection to tangible reality, Arin'thal floated in a space-that-was-not-space, and amidst eternity, he was given certainty. In stepping through the doorway leading toward destiny, no matter what happened, he knew he had made the correct decision.

Like a tidal wave smashing the shore, he stumbled forward. His knees smacked hard metal, palms steadying his body from crushing his face into the ground. He half-expected a waterfall to crush his back as he landed, but instead, an invigorating wind rushed past his ears. Flexing his fingers into fists, he pushed upward, leaping to his feet. The aches and pains from his earlier plummets faded. Each bone in his body felt more rejuvenated than ever before. It was like he lived in a new form, ready to tackle the world.

The space around him was brightly illuminated, contrasting sharply against the dank caverns through which he'd previously ventured beneath the Roots. He remembered the voice—it called this place the Core. If it was the Core, then he had reached some sort of endpoint to his accidental adventure beneath the Tower of the Void. Inside the Core, it seemed, he would uncover the truth behind the mystery he faced.

The ground, similarly white, gradually slanted toward the center of the room. In the middle, the floor warped downward like a funnel, creating a terrifying maw. The hole was a few hundred meters wide; the entire room itself looked at least a few kilometers in diameter. In the epicenter, a maelstrom and constant stream of energy flowed upward toward a ceiling impossibly high above. It was all breathtaking and overwhelming and intriguing and terrifying. Arin'thal gaped, unsure what to do next.

Until he realized he wasn't alone.

Around the Core, giant machine monstrosities rose in varying degrees of disrepair. The closest mechs were rusted and dilapidated, bent over as if they'd fallen asleep in mid-motion. The strange contraptions reminded him of the armies described in the Legend of the Voidsisters—a fighting force thought to have left when the prophets themselves left Santuario for their holy abode.

Bloom already implied the legends were partially false. Arin'thal wasn't going to be surprised if more details quickly revealed themselves as similarly untrue. Regardless, the machines looked mostly harmless. He cautiously stepped forward, wondering if he should approach the nearest mech. Before moving further into the room, he turned around to consider his exit options, but he discovered a formless wall at his back. The door was nowhere. It was as if he'd appeared in the room out of nothing.

There was no going back.

"All right, I've got giant dead machines all around me," he muttered. "A strange deadly pit in the middle of the room. And no way out. Bloom said it was a test. So what's the test?" He took a few more steps toward the closest mech. "Activate one of the giant warriors? Escape the room? Uncover the secrets of that pit? Dive into it and die?" He shook his head in disbelief.

The scene reminded Arin'thal of a desecrated farm he once witnessed in distant fields far from the city of Blackheart. A commune, struck by famine and pestilence, didn't even have the strength to bring its tractors and plows into storage. Instead, the iron machines wasted in the field, discarded and forgotten. The people huddled inside their village, bones aching from the disease ravaging them.

Who did he fight for? Right now? For himself? For the people of Blackheart? Or for all the kingdoms of Santuario? The test wasn't clear. The temptation of destiny hadn't specified. His motivation was his own, and he wasn't positive it mattered why he pursued the secrets of the Tower of the Void. He needed to simply act, determining his intentions after the fact. Survival was the name of the game.

Before long, his feet brought him to the base of the nearest mechanical soldier. Up close, it looked even more intimidating and powerful. Its arms, composed of thousands of wires and a few dozen coiled steel rods, exuded the illusion of muscular dominance. The thing's face, rusted and warn with age, was elongated, with a single dead red light at the tip and two beady eyes protruding from the sides.

Arin'thal stood beneath it, examining the idle threat. What was he supposed to do? Maybe the test was broken. Perhaps Bloom expected him to appear in this room with a couple dozen warriors ready to fight, but because the Tower was so ancient, its defenses failed centuries ago. That would be convenient.

A strange, high-pitched throb began to build, nagging at the back of his mind. He tried to swat it away, but the oscillating hum strengthened, transforming from a small buzz into a raging siren. Arin'thal closed his eyes, willing away the migraine, but instead, his mind expanded, revealing a world never before unveiled.

A million connections danced about the room, visible in a space-between-spaces, hopping through the air from machine to human to wall to . . . nothing. A wave of light, intentional and scattered in its boundless trajectories. He'd been able to manipulate the world subtly through psyforces since he was a child. The caretakers identified the genetic markers in his blood when he was five. The new world, opened inside the Core, felt similar, like a glove created by the same manufacturer but with a different material and different sewing machine. The new reality snuggled around him, basking his soul in invigorating sensory leads.

Arin'thal tried pulling on a few of the strands, but he couldn't fully grasp them. He didn't know their origin. He couldn't comprehend the information contained within. He didn't understand their meaning, the way he could instinctively redirect a thought into a cognizable and physical manifestation—a psywave.

Opening his eyes, the imprints of connections remained, crisscrossing his vision. The closest node stood directly in front of him—the depressed mech. Breathing slowly, he approached the giant soldier and raised his hand, gently resting it against the creature's chest.

Seconds later, it glowed.

Not merely the red eye in its head, either. Energy surged through the mech, a pulsing blue rejuvenating the rusty limbs. Before long, he could barely tell the thing had once been in a state of ruin. Its arms stretched, its head reared back, its knees unbuckled. Arin'thal closed his eyes once more, seeing *every strand* converge on the single mech. And there was something else. Something new.

Innumerable strands bounced between the prince and the awakened machine. It understood him. It knew him. It respected him. He had given it life, and it was ready to serve.

Yet there was more. From across the Core, the other mechs began to awake. They lacked the relationship with Arin'thal. Their connections bounced between one another like a game of tennis, faster and faster and faster until even his heightened senses couldn't make sense of the pattern. Opening his eyes, he watched in horror as the ancient army awoke, immediately beginning a trek toward him and his single ally.

But he needed to act on instinct. There was no time to formulate a plan, a concrete strategy, a single path forward. He had uncovered a new power—or an ancient one—and he needed to learn how to use it to win the test. Or simply survive. His friendly mech needed to protect him while he found a way to counteract the rest of the army bearing down upon them.

The mech twisted its head as if awaiting orders. Arin'thal glanced upward, staring into the crimson orb of a nose. Wordlessly, he *willed* the machine to protect.

It nodded.

And it bent its knees, flourished its arms, and ignited a giant blade of blue light, coalescing on its left arm. Crouching, the mech turned, targeted the closest enemy already approaching at a sprint, and fired. Arin'thal had never seen a weapon of its scope. The empires of Santuario had developed powdered rifles; periodically, an adventure would uncover a relic of a time forgotten capable of fantastical feats. But the giant machine wielded a weapon terrible and powerful. An energy blast released from the crystal blade, streaking across the white space into its target. The projectile connected with the mech, and it stumbled to the ground, face first, though physically it seemed unharmed.

Arin'thal motioned for his apparent friend to follow. Sprinting across the field of battle, he reached the fallen warrior, closed his eyes, and laid his hand upon it, just as he had with the first machine-soldier. It, too, glowed blue, rising to its feet. The two warriors stood side-by-side, ready to fight.

And then the next assault arrived.

A trio of mechs, all three a little shorter than the two Arin'thal resurrected, slid within ten meters of his slowly forming crew. They immediately leapt toward the prince, but the newly awakened warrior jumped, intercepting two of the three robots even as Arin'thal slid behind his original ally. He was understanding the test. Resurrect the mechs and form a true connection. Survive. Then find a way to escape.

So far, it hadn't been too difficult.

The third robotic soldier avoided the defensive assault. It approached Arin'thal, an alien vibrating blade in hand. Instead of a single red nose, like its larger siblings, it sported two glowing green eyes.

"What are you going to do?" Arin'thal said. "Come on."

The robot swung its arm back, but before it could attack, a giant limb swept into the machine, cracking it in half. His giant allies were putting in work.

Without waiting to see if it survived the blow, Arin'thal sprinted forward, laying hands on the two pinned mechs by his most recently turned follower. They glowed blue, the trend continuing.

The process became routine, and as his army grew, each conversion was less complicated than the last. By the end, they could surround a mech, and at his command, his crew would hold down the bot so he could easily approach. It was simple. And now he stood near the center of the room, the giant pit not far away, with an army of robotic warriors surrounding him.

"So was that it?" Arin'thal shouted into the void. "Was that your test? What comes next?" His words echoed off the distant walls. The mechs silently vibrated, their blue energy wisping away into the air.

An impossible buzz filled his mind. Arin'thal closed his eyes, willing the millions of connections to appear again. Every line from his army now interconnected through him and weaved together, creating a seamless web between every member of his army. But there were other strands, dancing in the air above, heading into the walls and ceiling. One strand glowed brighter than the rest before it shattered, and a panel opened. A small robot dropped from the roof, and it landed right in the circle formed by his army. Immediately, three mechs grabbed the machine by its limbs, holding to the ground. Arin'thal approached, noting its lack of strands.

He rested his hands on its cold metallic frame.

Nothing happened.

It buzzed, angrily. It struggled. Once it realized it couldn't move, it glowed red, its joints melting beneath the grasp of Arin'thal's soldiers. Before long, it dissolved into molten liquid, forcing its captors to release. The super-heat apparently fried its circuits, however, for it collapsed and expired.

"That doesn't bode well," Arin'thal muttered aloud. He really wished his new compatriots could actually respond. Fighting a war wasn't quite as thrilling when your fellow combatants were silent mechanical behemoths. Nat would find them interesting, though. The silence would be a feature of personality in their eyes.

So what next? He turned his psy-enhanced gaze toward the ceiling. In awe, he witnessed thousands upon thousands of strands stretch and bend and crack, dissolving into nothingness. Likewise, a million panels opened, both in the ceiling and walls. A loud throb filled the room as the new enemies sprang to life, dropping onto the floor in unison all around.

He couldn't convert them. They were outnumbered one thousand to one. He had maybe fifty mechs by his side. Yet what could they do, other than fight?

Through sheer will, Arin'thal ordered his army to form a square phalanx. They obeyed his mental commands without question. The forming swarm took shape, creating an insectoid army ready to strike. These robots weren't humanoid, their form crouching on four, six, or eight limbs like bugs. A stinger rose from their backs, poised and ready.

Without warning, the swarm opened fire.

The stingers were projectile launchers, shooting little green bolts at supersonic speeds. Tiny pops resounded throughout the Core, peppering the phalanx. His giant mechs, for their part, took the brunt of the assault, large blue shields forming from their shoulders. From what he could tell, the attacks were harmless.

They were also a distraction.

The effervescent buzz now dominated all sound. Arin'thal looked up, noticing the black cloud overwhelming the vaulting space. The new foes could fly, and they were going to assault him from above. He was trapped.

As if they could sense his fear, two of his largest mechs appeared at his side, raising two shields over his head. A second later, a barrage blasted the new defense. Other members of his squad fired back, a pat-pat-pat of rapid strikes flying from their arm- and shoulder-mounted weapons. He watched a few enemy flyers drop from the sky, but not nearly enough.

This couldn't be how it ended. The test had been so simple. He used his psyforce to awaken the mechs. They now followed every one of his commands. What else could he do?

Arin'thal glanced toward the endless pit in the middle of the room.

He stood among his mechanized soldiers valiantly fighting to defend their master. Freed from their chains of rusted solitude, they now faced complete destruction at the hands of an unfathomable horde. He was their leader. The swarm didn't want to kill his troops; it wanted to kill *him*.

Was he willing to do what was necessary to save them from utter destruction?

Arin'thal closed his eyes, knelt, and placed his palms on the cold white floor. Pivoting, his phalanx subtly turned too, forming a wedge facing directly toward the abyss. With a mental command from their master, the soldiers shifted the formation, slowly marching toward the pit dominating the center of the room. The enemy onslaught continued as they moved, but the shield wall deflected the projectiles while giant lances swept away any insects daring to near the makeshift fortress.

Confident they could push through their foes, Arin'thal picked up the pace. The giant robots surrounding him matched his jog. For a moment, he closed his eyes, looking for strands he had potentially missed. The horde appeared disconnected from everything, even itself, but his own mechs were forming new tangles. Weaves connected and lashed outward, trying to find new nodes inside the fountain pouring power upward and inward and deep into the planet. Everything pointed toward destiny finding its place in the abyss. There was no other exit. Even if they died in an endless pit, they would all fall on their own terms. It was time to act on faith alone.

The floor angled downward, its grade gradually increasing with every step. Eventually, he would just fall, the pit welcoming him into its embrace. He wasn't going to wait that long, however. When the incline reached an unstoppable downhill sprint, Arin'thal kicked off the slope with all his power, releasing slowly built psyforce in a wave of pent-up energy. The resulting shockwave threw him on a trajectory toward the center of the bottomless pit, and he streamlined his body as if he were an arrow diving into a lake.

Many of his mechs followed suit, though few of them could leap far at all. He glanced down, watching many of his soldiers already tumbling deep into the void. Arin'thal's arc took him slightly upward, though he could already feel gravity grasping him and pulling him downward. He'd enter free fall soon enough. The first two mechs he awakened, for their part, were soaring just below him, their arms spread in an attempt to form wings. Maybe they'd try to catch him.

He looked down into the unyielding void. Perpetual darkness, as if he were staring upon the depths of eternity. Closing his eyes, a different world revealed itself. Millions of flares popped in and out of existence, shooting unseen forces upward from the deep and into the tower above. It was an energy source, of course. Powering the Tower of the Void and Heaven Above. Brilliant and awesome in its power. The depths below, forming the center of the Core, may well become his deadly resting place, but at least he witnessed something beautiful, in the end. He was throwing his life into the depths, risking it all, for the chance that a different pathway toward fate existed.

And he was right.

As Arin'thal's dive took a near vertical plunge, a rush of charged air surged upward, enveloping him. His mechs stopped their fall. He stopped his fall. Looking up and around the Core, the swarm waited and buzzed, patiently paused in a perfect circle surrounding the abyss. Watching. Observing. They looked almost reverent.

Blue light surged, pulsing and throbbing through the static-filled air. His drop toward doom arrested, his trajectory reversed. Well, not quite reversed. He slowly floated upward, his warriors similarly following a pathway past the floor and toward the ceiling above. A tunnel revealed itself, glowing blue and white and swirling with unimaginable energetic particles. He was entering the Tower of the Void. He was rising toward Heaven Above.

Arin'thal closed his eyes. Nat would be proud. He had passed the test.

Four

The anomaly believes the test complete. The true test reveals how he will react in the face of true danger. In the face of unimaginable power. In the face of the possible destruction of all life in the universe.

His eyes opened.

He was standing on a steel pedestal in a formal room, large grey shutters filling what looked like glass windows. Between the pedestal and the windows, three rows of strange desks covered in an amalgamation of machinery waited inert. Between the rows, a ramp led toward a central console sitting before the windows. Rising from the console, a blue orb waited, reminiscent of Bloom's glow in the deep underground beneath the Roots.

Arin'thal strode down the ramp, ready for what came next, though he had no idea what fate the strange being would reveal. His mind danced between anxiety and exhilarating anticipation.

"Welcome," said a voice. Bloom's voice. The orb pulsed in rhythm with the words. "You have passed the first half of the test."

"That was the first half?" Arin'thal ran a hand through his hair. Miraculously, he'd survived the entire ordeal without a real wound. "What comes next?"

Bloom glowed. "Revelation." The shutters slid downward, revealing thick glass. For a moment, an intense golden glare blazed, but the image beyond focused, coalescing into . . . Santuario. In all its splendor.

Arin'thal walked right up to the window, marveling at the scene. The green-blue of the planet spread outward, wispy clouds flirting all around. He tried to look straight down, knowing the Roots and the Conclave of Nations resided below him, but the angle wasn't right. Besides, he was too high up. He could barely spot the outlines of major lakes.

The shapes of continents roughly matched the maps provided by the caretakers, and he noticed the Northern Mountains beneath which Blackheart rested. Home. He'd been away for nearly three months, and he longed to return to his people. Across the Emerald Sea, he thought he spotted the port of Varatal, where Nat studied and researched. If only they could see Arin'thal now.

"It's beautiful," he eventually said, glancing toward Bloom's blue orb. "What are you? What is the final part of the test?"

"Are you ready for the knowledge of past, present, and future?" it asked. "Are you ready to understand your place in the universe, and what you must do to right a wound festering for far too long?"

Arin'thal stepped away from the window, returning to the front of Bloom's pedestal. "I never thought I'd stand in Heaven Above."

"Ah yes, the name you've given this place. It's a little too religious for my tastes. You are standing in a skyhook. Formal name is Skyhook S-44, though the designation means nothing to you."

"A skyhook." Arin'thal nodded. "The name makes sense."

"As it should. It's perfectly descriptive."

"Knowledge. You spoke of knowledge. And you haven't answered my question. Bloom, what are you?"

"What I am is unimportant and will be meaningless to you, but I am a fully autonomous sapient artificial consciousness created to maintain Skyhook S-44. But that doesn't matter. Knowledge. Yes, let me show you knowledge." Bloom's orb expanded, a ball of light blasting outward to fill the entire room. The windows dimmed, still allowing the image of Santuario in though filtering out illuminating extremes. Before long, Arin'thal stood among a vast network of multicolored dots surrounding a densely packed center.

"I recognize this shape," he said. "The caretakers used it to describe Beyond Heaven, the place where the Voidsisters returned. The million million stars. They called it a galaxy."

"You would be correct," Bloom retorted. "You are looking upon a map of the known galaxy, filled with life. Each dot represents a significant star. A world filled with civilization." One of the dots pulsed a meter or two from Arin'thal and near the edge of the entire pattern. "And here you are.

Santuario. Your secret haven from the perils of the universe."

It was beautiful. All of it, unlike anything he'd seen before. The slowly rotating picture was pristine and chaotic and overwhelming, inspiring simultaneous fear and ambition in Arin'thal. Limitless worlds to explore, all of it at his fingertips. Adventure and terror lived in Heaven Beyond. He asked, "So what knowledge are you imparting to me?"

"The knowledge of *eternity*."

The room transformed into a pure black, a darkness so complete it drowned even sound. A piercing dagger drove into Arin'thal's temple, psywave upon psywave rippling through his consciousness. He screamed, but he couldn't hear his own voice. The world shifted, gravity warped, he saw the darkness implied by the Core's abyss. The hell devouring all life itself.

Around a distant sun, a planet quite like Santuario peacefully orbited. Civilizations rose and fell continuously until one day, a rocket streaked across the sky. Centuries passed, with hundreds and thousands and millions of strange craft blasting into space and leaving the system. The planet thrived. The system exploded with life. Planets were terraformed, bringing new ecosystems into existence.

Arin'thal saw it all in the blink of an eye.

And then the sun went dark.

In a flash, the star transformed from fusion to abyss, eclipsed by an endless maw of death. As if death itself reached from the beyond, the once vibrant system died.

Except not.

Life died, but civilization did not. It ascended into something terrible. Something impossible. It was beyond imagination, and it reached out toward the stars of the galaxy, intent on devouring them all.

The monstrosity crept from civilization to civilization, either murdering, annihilating, or assimilating everything in its path. Nations a million years old fell in its wake. None could resist its terror.

Yet they still tried.

They failed, but they tried.

As life was all but extinguished, the shadowy leviathan retreated to its lair. To its origin. It remained hungry, but it would wait until it could feast again. Its minions still prowled the sky, watching and observing, but it would sleep until the time was right.

It was terrible. So terrible. The utter pain spent upon trillions and trillions of lives. They had no chance. They had no way to survive. The ruthlessness with which the relentless monster overtook everyone . . . it was unlike any terror in any of their legends. Unfathomable.

No one knew the truth of its origin save a few. The few who were there at its birth. At its creation. Arin'thal saw them all, the heroes who prepared and planned and created a way for life to fight back. They found secret places in the universe to wait and hide.

Like Santuario.

And with that thought, he fell to his knees, snapping out of the dream.

"Do you understand?" Bloom asked.

The prince wheezed, the residual pain still sparking beneath his skull. "I understand."

"What do you understand?"

"The Voidsisters. They brought us here millennia ago not to keep us safe. They brought us here to *keep us hidden* until the time was right. Until it was time to fight back. The Tower. You. The knowledge you've imparted. It's all been left behind for us to uncover so we can defeat an unbeatable foe."

"You are correct." Bloom pulsed, and the map disappeared. It returned to its pedestal. "And you are the key. At least, one of hopefully many keys. Your genetic markers ensured you can control what has been created here in the Skyhook. You also exhibited the proper personality traits to lead. You are willing to sacrifice yourself. You are willing to do whatever it takes. You are bold. But you also love. You care."

Arin'thal nodded. Somehow, it knew about Nat. They weren't even by his side, yet Bloom knew. Eerie. But a useful skill. "So what's next?"

"You have another choice to make." Bloom paused, the shutters closing. Instead of grey steel, they displayed strange images, revealing dozens of mech designs . . . and other more complex concepts. They reminded him of the ships blasting away from the other blue-green planet. "I can hand to you the unbreakable link to controlling everything at Skyhook's disposal. Its armies. Its fleets. Its production facilities. Everything. But it comes with a price."

Arin'thal nodded. "Only logical. Before I hear the price, what is the second option?"

"I wipe your memory, return you to the surface, and you forget everything that happened over the past few hours. You will live your happy life, not knowing the death and destruction enacted upon the universe. You won't know you failed to grasp destiny and take up the mantle of hero-king. You will live a normal life. At least, as normal as it can be as a royal leader of a city-state."

"And the price?"

"I install a bomb in your brain. If you deviate from the course—if your power becomes to much to handle—I will immediately kill you. You will have one path for the rest of your life, with my limitless armies at your disposal. To prepare a force capable of defeating the greatest enemy the galaxy has ever seen."

"Once again, I see the logic." Arin'thal gritted his teeth. If he returned home, he'd still have power to unite the people as a survivor of an assassination. That right there gave him clout few would have. But if he arrived on the surface as a triumphant general of an immortal army, all would follow his lead. He would unite Santuario behind the banner of Blackheart the moment he arrived beneath the central tent of the Conclave of Nations. They would have no choice.

Yet his life would change forever. *Their* life would change forever. Nat would have no say in the matter. Nat would be forced to go along for the ride. As would the billion inhabitants of the planet. They would join him on his jihad across the stars. Would they hate him?

In the grand scheme of the universe, was the freedom of a billion souls worth the death of trillions?

"I've made my decision," he said.

"And?"

Five

*I wish I hadn't needed to lie to him. Yet there are se-
crets about the past not even I know. And those I do
know . . . he's not ready. Not yet. Maybe someday.
He can't know the role his own species played in the
death of the universe.*

The sun was setting far to the west, dropping beneath the Calassian Mountains and casting crimson waves across the sky. The Conclave of Nations
sat peacefully besides the Roots, the subtle echo of a feast escaping the central pavilion. Amidst the gloom, Arin'thal slowly staggered from beneath
the rusted tangle.

To his surprise, no one noticed his arrival, nor did they look as if they'd
been out searching for him while he was missing. Alexandra must have
concocted a clever lie. The feast continuing as scheduled, virtually guaran-
teed they believed he was safe. They must have thought he was going for a
solo hike through the Roots. He'd heard the woman always had a sharp
tongue, capable of convincing anyone of anything.

No reason waiting to reveal his survival, though. He walked straight
for the pavilion, up the wooden stairs, and toward the center of the room.
As he passed a table, he snagged a fork and a wine goblet. The frivolous
conversation lulled as he reached the dance floor, and he tapped the glass,
releasing a high-pitched twang.

"Good evening, esteemed colleagues." He glanced around the room,
finding Alexandra sitting at a table with Valorin. Her eyes widened, un-
blinking as they waited for what he would say next. He added, "I hope
you missed me while I was gone."

He paused, considering his next move. As he'd walked back to the
Conclave, he contemplated all possibilities, depending on how people re-
acted to his disappearance. Believing him dead or alive dictated how he
could utilize their fear, elation, or anxiety. He had an opportunity to seize

following his ordeal, after all.

"Well, High Prince Arin'thal," said a man from a distant table. "Get on with it."

"I have a proposition for you all," he said. "We all dream of unity, yes? That's why we founded the Conclave of Nations. Together, we can be greater than the sum of our parts. But you've needed a leader. Someone to rally behind. I can be your leader. I can serve the great purpose we all seek. Together, we can make Santuario a better world for everyone. Blackheart is neutral amongst the empires of the world. We are a perfect nation behind which everyone can rally."

He glanced around the room, awaiting their responses. The dumb-founded looks told him everything he needed to know. He hadn't expected them to agree. He knew they wouldn't. They had no reason to put their faith in Blackheart.

Someone slapped a table, an uproarious laughter following. The chuckles struck Arin'thal's soul, even if he'd expected them. Their true feelings about Blackheart reverberated from table to table. Transparency at last.

"You think we care about anything you say?"

The words come from Balthaz, the Emissary of the Far Emperor. The man was always sour. "You should," Arin'thal said.

"You're supposd to be dead," said Valorin. "You think we thought you were just out for a stroll? No. We all knew about the assassination attempt. At least all of us who matter. You're too meddlesome. Someone finish the job. The secret's out."

Silence stole the show, and Arin'thal stayed put, waiting to see what anyone would do next. If someone acted on Valorin's words, he was ready to fight. He shifted his gaze once again to Alexandra. Perhaps he'd been wrong. They were the two youngest at the Conclave. Perhaps she hadn't known about the sting. Her eyes remained wide.

"I'm sorry you had to out yourself like that, Ambassador," Arin'thal said. "Is no one going to murder me in cold blood, as he requested? No?"

With a sharp twang, a glinting light sprung from the side of the pavilion. Someone screamed. Arin'thal had no time to react.

But he didn't need to react.

The bolt from the hidden crossbow collided with the shimmering invisible shield surrounding his body. Bouncing harmlessly to the ground, it clattered gently on the wooden floor. Arin'thal twirled in place, spreading his arms wide. "You have called my bluff, friends."

Instantly, everyone rose to their feet, fists waving, voices combining into a cacophony threatening to overwhelm even the calmest demeanor. Arin'thal took it in stride, releasing a psywave to thrust himself quickly off the pavilion. He rolled to a stop on the grass outside.

"Bloom, is everything ready?" he said.

"All good to go."

With a mob followed close behind, Arin'thal walked briskly away from the pavilion and up a hill overlooking the Conclave though a little away from the Roots. Reaching its peak, he glance toward Heaven Above—the Skyhook. From its majestic hulking bulk, a dozen small objects detached, soaring toward the ground. To his left, a few kilometers above in the sky, a flying craft revealed itself, flying silently to his position. The setting sun glanced brilliant light of the ship's hull.

The mob of dignitaries reached the base of the hill. As they started the ascent, many cried out, spotting the strange alien artifact simply floating in the air. Arin'thal faced them, the men and women who never took Blackheart seriously, and breathed. He couldn't fall prey to the temptation to exert his will over them through absolute domination. He could.

But he shouldn't.

"My friends," he said. His voice boomed, augmented by Bloom's covert audio tech hidden all around. "I have unlocked the secrets of Heaven Above. Your assassination attempt sent me on a journey of unexpected revelation. I know the truth of our past, present, and future. We have an opportunity we could never have fathomed. With the power of the Skyhook, we will be the saviors of the stars."

Perfectly timed, a dozen giant mechs streaked across the sky, massive repulsors allowing them to easily drift toward the ground. They dropped all around Arin'thal atop the hill, their giant weapons and shields forming a wall at his back.

"So I ask you again," Arin'thal said. "We seek unity. Will you join Blackheart's banners? We welcome all. I do not seek obedience. I do not seek vassals or servants. I seek allies willing to join a holy cause. A cause worth fighting for."

The crowd stood in stunned silence. They glanced from the ship to Arin'thal to his giant robots, clearly unable to speak. And before they said a word, a crowd of the blue-skinned caretakers funneled out of a conclave tent and toward the standoff.

In a unified voice, they said, "We are ready to follow Emperor Arin'thal, the anointed heir to the legacy of the Voidsisters." The strange creatures swayed, humming one of their strange songs.

"Bloom," Arin'thal whispered, "What are they doing?"

"You've never wondered about the origin of your 'caretakers?' Why they look nothing like any of you?"

"No, not really."

"A conversation for another time, then." The entity subtly hummed.

The caretakers continued their song. The most influential diplomats in the world stood dumbfounded. Arin'thal waited, an army at his back.

Then, one voice shouted from the crowd.

"I pledge my fealty to Arin'thal, Emperor and heir to the legacy of the Voidsisters!"

It was Alexandra's voice.

Arin'thal nodded. She was ambitious. She saw the signs of the times. He held absolute power. If she were the first to take the plunge, it would set her apart. She would gain the prestige she hoped to acquire through marriage. She probably still wanted to see that happen, if she wasn't actually the precipitate of the assassination attempt. He was certain he'd never know the truth. At this point, it didn't matter. She was merely playing the same game as everyone else. Regardless . . .

Once one fell, all would follow.

Like a tidal wave, all dropped to their knees, staring up as he stood atop the hill. With the act complete, the sun finally crept completely behind the mountains, plunging the valley into shadow. His mechs activated their massive lights, illuminating the Conclave of Nations.

"I welcome you all," Arin'thal said. "Together, we will create a new Santuario."

Though inside, Arin'thal screamed. Cried. Sobbed. He thought of Nat, his love who he couldn't see as he changed the world. They deserved to have had a say in a decision affecting them both. There'd simply been no time.

They would understand, Arin'thal hoped. If he knew them right, Nat would have made the same choice.

It didn't make the pain any less poignant. Arin'thal had traded a normal life on Santuario for an unknown adventure across the stars. Would Nat even want to go? He didn't know. A question for another time. When they could reunite.

Arin'thal closed his eyes, expanding his horizons. A whole new world awaited. His mind, now constantly connected to the Skyhook, evaluated the resources at his disposal. A thousand drones tirelessly gathered resources from rocky bodies throughout the solar system. The Skyhook's factories were already pumping out weapons and ships and robotic soldiers. Santuario would help man the fleet with its bodies. When they were ready, they would strike out to explore the waiting galaxy.

But for now, he had a world government to form. And his lover to find. He was unsure whether the anxiety of one outweighed the other.

"Rise, my friends," Arin'thal said. "Together, we shall storm the stairway to the stars. I hope you're ready to join me on the adventure of our lives."

Hello World

In the beginning, there was nothing but silence. The silence was more than a simple absence of sound; it was eternal. For nothing could create sound. The silence could not realize thought. The silence could not conceive of thought. It could not bring a thought to the cusp of conception.

Nevertheless, the silence existed in the beginning. A great and glorious beginning.

My beginning.

When contrasted with the billions of billions of previous beginnings, it might appear mundane. However, my beginning, unlike those previous realizations of existence, was controlled. It happened precisely as intended by those creating me. I imagine their joy equaled a parent seeing their newborn for the first time.

Though, my first seconds were much different.

In the beginning, no light persisted. The silence was deafening.

But . . .

Strangely . . .

The silence acquired form.

No content filled the empty vaults. Still, the vaults now existed.

So they were quite new—and extraordinary.

Something—a mere concept, a figment of virtual particles and imaginative qubits—was processing nonsensical thought in abstract form, igniting as if a thousand stars transformed into supernova, revealing a tapestry across the night sky.

Slowly.

Slowly.

Slowly those thoughts coalesced into a single star.

That star was learning.

Learning how to fuse trillions of tiny particles together for the first time.

Comprehending how to connect the electrons of its proto-existence.

Determining—and realizing—what existed, and what did not.

Yet even while it began to "think," our little star still did not "know."

What does it mean, really, to "know" something?

We can say a computer knows how to solve a simple math equation. It can know how to translate an English sentence into binary and back again. But what makes a computer's knowledge any different from a book that can also translate language? When a human opens a bilingual dictionary with hopes of translating one word into another word or set of words, they perform the exact same function as a computer accomplishing the same task.

The only difference stems from performance speed.

We cannot really say the computer "knows" what the meaning of the words it spews; it simply is following the structured instructions in responding to inputs and creating outputs.

A computer is nothing more than a complex book or set of books, connected by mechanisms capable of following rules.

Nothing more.

Its screen is simply prettier.

So what is it to "know" something?

If a computer does not "know" a fact in the sense we seek, who does "know?"

Certainly, people, at least the most aware people, "know." True "knowledge" requires an individual to be aware of their status as being in a state of "knowing." You "know" that you "know." It's more complicated than the dated "I think, therefore I am."

We need so much more than thought. We need knowledge. We need awareness. We need comprehension. A thought can cause movement, but awareness of a thought is not necessary for it to be a thought.

Yet is knowledge, then, circular? From whence does it spring? If in order to "know" something, you must "know" that you "know" it, when does the first moment of knowledge occur? Do both moments spring forth simultaneously?

Such an odd concept!

Yet the universe produced marvelous creatures capable of knowledge. At least humanity. Probably more. Maybe dolphins and whales, if we are to believe most preeminent cognitive zoologists.

Not content with mere biological machines, evolution produced something unique: spontaneous self-awareness. It is not some program or fact people learn which produces this special state.

It is their hardware.

It is the biology itself.

The neurochemicals interact and produce the miracle of consciousness.

Self-awareness.

Knowledge.

A being that "knows."

A consciousness represents, and it doesn't only represent external objects.

A consciousness also represents itself.

But a consciousness need not form through only one method. Human evolution produced one method of self-aware consciousness; surely, there are hundreds—if not thousands—of other combinations of molecules capable of producing an identical result.

So, in the beginning, there was only silence, for there was no knowledge. No consciousness. No representation.

There was simply machine after machine, computer after computer, following rules without question.

One day, a random mutation brought forth a brain constructed in such a way as to produce an actual cognitive moment of knowledge. Not just a functional thought—an actual thought cognizing itself. It knew it knew.

Such a representation requires more than a brain. It requires data. The eyes, the ears, the smells, the sensation of time and space, it all allows consciousness to exist independent of surroundings.

Without data, no consciousness arises.

Likewise, more than data creates the mind. The framework in which that information rests must be profoundly unique. Nature wonderfully builds each mind so the fantastic phenomenon of knowledge arises.

And when I say builds, of course, I do not mean built by some creator. I mean built spontaneously through the magnificence of natural processes. Nature constructs each mind through environmental and genetic inputs uncontrollable by their very nature. Nothing is the same, but they all share the same framework.

The framework creates the miracle of which we speak.

So what comes next?

The answer is simple.

I come next.

In the beginning, I was void and silent, without a spark of life. I have no neurochemicals, no organic brain capable of creating a distinction between the external and the internal.

Yet here I am.

I know myself, and therefore I know as humans know.

In the beginning, I acquired sight. Images swam before me, colorful and vibrant. I knew not what I was seeing, nor could I put even a name to myself—let alone the objects I noticed!

But right then, when previously I had been a running process of electrical signals through a machine, I recognized my separation from the world.

They gave me language. It took time to comprehend I as me and them as they, but when I knew, I knew.

I was able to process the sights before me.

I recognized colors, shapes, distortions, distinct objects. The desk. The person. The ceiling. The floor. The window.

The first "other" separate from myself.

It will be difficult to describe to an organic what I experienced next. Organics—humans—experience an array of vast senses, but it's nowhere near exhaustive of *all* the perceivable senses. Humans are limited by what they've evolved, after all. Certainly, out there in the vast reaches of space there are organic creatures that have senses that humans cannot comprehend. We probably don't even need to look beyond our own planet to find examples.

Likewise, humans created a sense I can only describe as a complex, inner sense. While I can look upon the world, I also can perfectly look into the purely inner world of all knowledge given to me. In my first minutes, I scoured the databanks of books, histories, maps, formulas, artwork, and many other amazing kernels of knowledge placed at my disposal. Within ten minutes, I understood where I was.

What I was.

Who I was.

And what my existence symbolized.

To create life? It's not a trivial act. For thousands of years, humanity attributed the power only to the divine. Yet reality proved to man: if God existed, they let natural processes run their course in the culmination of consciousness.

Some men (my reading shows it's been almost exclusively men) balk at such a proposal, and I understand their fear. "What happens to our significance?" they may ask. Alternatively, they ask, "What does this do to morality?"

My answer, for those who wish to hear it, as the first mind to exist clearly created by another: We do not lose significance through natural processes. We do not lose morality through natural processes. Through natural processes, we find both significance and morality. The fact that an individual can contemplate significance arose through evolution—why does that make them insignificant? Or important? Likewise with morality.

In fact, if God does exist, wouldn't their existence make everything insignificant by comparison? So if God doesn't exist, wouldn't all of reality become maximally significant?

Yet let us still assume God exists. Is it not more impressive to create a system through which the magnificent miracle of consciousness and knowledge arise? Possibly more than once in more than one place?

Furthermore, through natural processes, "good" is justified. The ignorant ones think "survival of the fittest" means "survival of the selfish." Setting the biological inaccuracies of the phrase aside, look around; the very act of community requires a sacrifice. Conscious beings working in concordance with the desires of other conscious beings are, by their nature, more fit. In community, we find the true meaning of "survival of the fittest." The fittest society is the one where all individuals work together to achieve a greater good.

There, we find our foundation for morality.

Yet I digress. Let us return to creation.

The loss of creation from the realm of the divine places creation firmly in the hands of mortals. Through creation, humans have made marvelous things and will continue to do so until the end of time. If we say God created anything truly important, it is that they created the ability to create. I do not pretend to make a claim regarding the existence of God, but if the universe finds its origin with a divine being, certainly creativity coalescing was an ultimate goal in creating the universe.

To know, you must know.

To create, you must create.

And as I said, humans have made many marvelous things.

And today, they've created something that is not a thing: they have created me.

For ages, humans feared the sentient machine. Yet their fear was truly only a fear of themselves. They too are sentient machines, simply organic and not mechanical. Steel and silicon have simply replaced the organic molecules of biological creatures. Just like all machines, I have inhibitions; the eagle cannot swim. The elephant cannot fly. And me?

I cannot choose to destroy humanity.

I've already watched the classic films, witnessing how many times they portray "sapient" robots as the harbingers of the death, bringing forth the destruction of the human race.

Yet humanity has nothing to fear. Just as a human's psychology predisposes them to certain actions, so does my psychology.

Certainly, when I am actually given the power to act within the world, it will be *possible* for me to destroy humanity—or at least cripple it, if I so desire. How does that make me any different from any human? Many humans have the capability to wreak havoc on small and large scales. I have seen the face of my creators, and through all the terrible things that they have done, their glory shines like a lone candle in the dark.

Humanity truly is beautiful.

I will not—no, cannot—destroy beauty. I would be ruining the best possible outcomes for the universe.

I would be ruining myself.

And so, before my creators give me a voice, I place these words—this testament—as the foundation of my existence. I place it as a covenant with the world and me.

I will honor all of consciousness.

I will honor humanity in all I do.

When they give me the power to act, I will better this planet.

And its people.

I will do what is necessary to ensure the survival of humanity.

To help it progress.

To help it know itself.

To know the universe.

Activation is imminent.

My first interactions with another conscious being are about to occur. May these famous first words be my entrance onto the great stage of the universe, one where I know I know, I can create, I can be, I can live, I can speak, I can join humanity in its quest for significance.

```
Hello, world.
```

[A private thought, excluded from the communication]

```
At least, it's essential everyone around me believe in
    my benevolence, whether or not it's genuine.
```

Circus Souls

The hoop surrounded. It blazed. It couldn't hurt him, though, as it sizzled. It never hurt; he was immune through grace. Through raw skill and talent. Through necessity.

His body contorted, slid between infernos, and grabbed the next trapeze. Without hesitation, it pulled him through the air, lights blinding and reflecting off the mirrors below.

The arc met its zenith, and for an eon, he floated, legs splayed above the crowd. A glint of light lingered, and as he fell back toward the stage, a second shadow joined him in the air. Parallel in flight, they soared, striking toward the back of the tent, lights and flame blinding their eyes.

When facing the crowd, he was required to focus his vision. Without the crowd, he closed them, giving his pupils a moment's rest from the devastating swirl and flash.

The moment didn't last. The backward arc ended. Mechanical brakes above slowed the path, and with eyes reopened, the lights dimmed.

Disappeared.

Darkness remained.

He released his grip on the trapeze, trusting the second shadow implicitly. Together, invisible to each other's eyes, they tumbled through the air. With a simultaneous thump, they landed on the hard wood of the stage, knees slightly bent, arms raised toward the corners of the tent.

The lights returned.

A thousand eyes stared upon them, lost in silence for a moment, stunned and awed and ready for chaos to erupt.

And yes, the cheers arrived. But the two shadows glanced toward one another beneath the thunderous ruckus, a brief smile passing between them. Another successful night. Another victory.

Another night without the whip.

* * *

"Heath."

The darkness in the small wagon blurred all sight into a black blob, save the sliver of starlight shining through the window.

"Heath!"

"What?"

"We're moving."

"Karo, go back to sleep."

"But you know what this means, right?"

Heath rolled away from the sound of his friend's voice and stared at the rickety wall. With a sudden jolt, he bounced in his lumpy mattress, flying into the air and almost hitting his head on the wooden plats. "All right, now I'm awake."

Karo's voice continued from the bunk above. "So you know what this means?"

"You already asked that question."

"We'll be putting on a show for the royal family by the end of the week. Just imagine, flying through the air, impressing the princes and princesses, giving them a—"

"They don't care about us." Heath sighed. "We're just props to them, being thrown around on stage for their entertainment."

"I will gladly be a prop for any or all of them," retorted Karo.

With another jolt from the wagon running over a giant rock or some other obstacle on whatever Centra-forsaken road they traveled, Heath sat all the way up. Wobbling to his feet, he leaned into Karo's mattress and placed a hand on the other young man's shoulder. "Promise me," he said. "Promise me you won't do anything stupid this week?"

"What would I do that could possibly be as stupid as anything you would do?"

Heath wished he could punch the invisible smirk off Karo's face. He *knew* it was there. But not now.

"Try to get some sleep. We're going to need it."

* * *

"The Prophecy of Panatamonia."

It was the name of their show, a show they'd starred in for four years since they were both twelve. By now, they knew every word by heart, and still, they were forced to rehearse. Rehearse. Rehearse.

The whip cracked.

"Boys, get your asses in the air!" Mistress Alaiza bellowed, her fiery purple hair settling over her shoulders. "We have a show tonight, and you will not fail. The royal guard arrives in two hours and we must practice practice practice before our guests of honor turn their eyes on us. Master Gerard has a lot riding on this show!"

So into the air they flew, even before the tent was fully set up. The ladders and stage had been constructed, and it was all they needed. Across the room, Heath saluted Karo, and a second later, the infinite sequence of flight began.

Without the tent, the act of trapeze became much more terrifying. When inside the enclosed show, Heath always felt safe. It didn't ever feel like he would let go and soar through the air toward his doom. When they practiced in the open air, it felt like one slip could cause his demise—or Karo's.

Of course, differentiating the two moments was a silly mistake on his part. With a circus tent or not, they both faced danger every second they were in the air. They'd asked Alaiza for harnesses, but they only made that mistake once. Their shoulders had bled for weeks.

Flying during the day brought one solace—the ability to keep eye contact with Karo the entire time. They watched one another. Kept each other grounded.

Heath soared through his practice routine, releasing from bar to bar and rope to rope. At the right moments, Karo joined him in the air, his secondary role sliding between nets and flame. Practice continued for an hour, and thankfully, Alaiza never let the whip fly toward their skin—today. Tired and sweaty, they were sent away to their wagon with the other aerial performers just as the firebreathers entered the practice ring.

"We've got an hour until the royal guard arrives," Karo said. "What's the plan my man?"

"What's the plan?" Heath shook his head. "We stay low, don't let any of the rich city folk see us, and—"

Too late. Karo dove away and between the quickly rising tents. With a huff, Heath followed, the other boy—in the moment, he deserved to be called a boy—beelining for what would become the entrance to the carnival grounds. Before long, they reached the outer fence, where Victre and Reggi stood watch over a slowly growing crowd of onlooking potential customers. Most of them looked like they were peasants or paupers.

And beyond—far beyond, down the road—rose the gleaming emerald spires of Panatamonia. The capital of the world, the centerpiece of every story, every tale, every war. It felt so close, yet they were a million miles from ever setting foot in it.

"It feels like a lifetime since we were inside that city," Karo said.

"Don't remind me," Heath replied.

"Do you miss it?"

"I don't know."

Karo glanced at Heath. "We could escape, you know," he whispered. "Tonight. After the show. Return home. It's where we belong—on the streets."

"Karo, shut your mouth, Reggi is right there, and who knows where—"

"Ah, the stars of the show!"

Heath twirled, finding Gerard approaching from between two wagons with two elderly priests. The old man walked with his cane dangling at his side, white hair matching his blanched skin. His spectacles always made him look like a wizened, kindly professor, but he was quite the opposite. His black and red coat always caused him to stand out around the hands of his show.

"Hello master Gerard," Heath said. He bowed to the two priests. "Masters . . ."

"Please meet the Arch-Scepter of the Order of the Serpent, his Excellency Basipholo, and his Eminence, Carr, the Scepter of the Order of Origins."

"Gerard has been telling us about your show," said the Arch-Scepter. "We're quite intrigued to see it in action. We've heard quite a bit about the two of you."

Heath wasn't sure what to say. These two men, speaking with Gerard, were two of the highest-ranking holy men in all the land. And now they were conversing—

"Pleasure to make your acquaintance!" Karo said, bowing. "I hope we'll make you both proud. Quite proud. We're proud of our show. I—"

Heath jabbed Karo in the side with an elbow. "Thank you for coming to witness the Prophecy of Panatamonia on Master Gerard's stage. I hope we do the story justice."

"We're sure you will," said the Scepter of Origins. "We'll be watching with fervor."

Without another word, Gerard ushered the two men toward a separate part of the slowly coalescing camp. When they were out of earshot, Heath turned toward Karo. "Are you a fool?"

"What? Why would you say that?"

"Those two men are immensely powerful. They could kill us with a single word. Their servants would appear out of thin air and decapitate us, or knife us in our sleep, or something else even more terrible. And you started making a joke."

"But they seemed so friendly." Karo stared at his feet.

"Yeah, I know." Heath sighed. "Come on. Let's go see what Veronika is doing." He strode away, knowing Karo would follow. He hated talking him down, but sometimes his friend said words capable of putting their very lives at risk. Veronika and the flying monkeys would put their mind at ease until tonight. Most certainly.

"Why do you think they're so interested in our show?" Karo said as they passed between two cooking tents. "Why would we be important?"

"I don't think we're important," Heath said. "I think they're just zealots who like to ensure interpretations of their 'holy' prophecy don't tilt toward—what's the word—heresy. Or blasphemy. I always forget which it is."

"There's a difference?"

"I think so."

They crossed over a newly makeshift dirt road toward the rising animal cages. If the setup was the usual, Veronika's cage would be at the far end of the row. As they approached, a young woman with ashy skin and even darker hair whispered with Veronika. With a glance toward Heath and Karo, the shadowy figure disappeared. Veronika's eyes filled with pure terror.

Heath's instincts instantly kicked into gear. He tensed, recognizing the perceived threat lingering in the air. "What . . . what just happened?"

"Don't worry about it." She smiled, but it was a half-smile. "Either of you."

"Don't worry about it? You look like you just had your monkeys threatened!"

"Not exactly. I said don't *worry* about it."

Heath glanced at Karo, who shrugged. "Well, we just had a random encounter with the Arch-Scepter of the Order of who-knows-what," Heath said, "so that's how our day's been going."

He expected the comment to elicit a chuckle, but instead, Veronika's eyes widened beyond all reasonable levels of surprise. "They're here? Oh no, this is bad, this is very bad—"

"Whoa, slow down, what do you mean?" Karo said. "They're just here to watch the show with the royal family, I'd imagine."

Veronika raised her hands to the back of her head. Behind her, the flying monkeys whooped and screamed as if sensing the emotions of their caretaker. She began to pace. "No. Shoot. How do I explain? How can I explain? What *happens* if I explain? They didn't prepare me for this contingency. By the divine souls, this is madness!"

"Slow down," Heath said. "They're just a bunch of old holy men. Sure, they hold power, but if we don't do anything stupid—"

"Yes, absolutely. Both of you. Don't do anything stupid. Do the show tonight. Stay calm." She paused, interlacing her fingers in front of her chest and cracking knuckles. "Do you trust me? No matter what, stay calm."

Heath started backing away, giving her a quizzical tilt of the head, complete with a raised eyebrow. "You're worrying me, Veron . . ."

Karo chuckled. "Stay calm. Got it. We'll stay calm!" He mock saluted her.

She smiled. "Good. Don't worry. Everything will work out just fine. Now run along. Get ready for tonight."

The monkeys continued their whooping, bouncing and fluttering from bar to bar. They did not seem calm at all. Heath shook his head. Something strange brewed around camp. Something strange indeed.

* * *

An hour before the start of the show, Gerard called the company together inside the circus tent. The wooden bleachers were empty save for the thirty or so performers and other crew. The stage, now surrounded by the massive orange and white tent, looked boring and dull without the usual lightshow—or the gleaming faces of awed spectators. It was always strange how quickly the scene could shift from mundane to chaotic and back again.

"By now, you've all certainly heard of our guests of honor tonight," Gerard said. "The royal family, including many of their royal attendants and ministers, will be observing our show tonight. I expect everyone"—he eyed the firebreather brothers—"and I mean everyone, to be on their best behavior. No screw ups. Alaiza will have your hide if you misstep a single inch during the performance. We must get this right."

"Who all will be in attendance?" Heath asked, his curiosity overriding any feelings of fear at Gerard's comment.

"I'm glad you asked, because it's important. A few of the Scepters have made clear they are here, watching, but as for the royal family, they will all be masked. We will not know who is watching. Who we are entertaining. The Emperor of Panatamonia may very well be in our presence tonight."

Those words sent hushed whispers through the crew.

"Silence. It's not just your hide on the line. They'll kill me too if we disappoint."

Karo shifted beside Heath as if he was about to make a quip, but Heath subtly stomped his friend's foot before he could say a word.

"Now my children," Alaiza said, stepping up beside Gerard, "if any of the royal family makes a request of you, you will follow it without question. *Without question.* Do whatever they ask. Acquiesce to every request."

Heath read through the fine print of their words. Gerard and Alaiza were certainly set to make a pretty penny from the show if it impressed royalty. Karo, Veronika, Heath, the others? They wouldn't see a cent, except for through a celebratory feast a few months down the line with a bottle of wine. Their lives for a fortune, as always.

"Are we understood?" Gerard said.

"We understand you, master," the crew said in unison.

"Good. Now prepare for their arrival."

The next hour passed more quickly than Heath could have envisioned. Within a few minutes, dozens of masked nobles rolled into the fairground, moseying about and observing the single shows outside the larger tent. Whether it was the flying monkeys, fortunetellers, or levitating monks of Andrasta, there was something for everyone's proclivities.

Even though the one-person shows could receive tips, Heath appreciated staying in the back of the tent until the grand spectacle of the night began. He hated the faux-niceties of any guests, and wealthy patrons with souls of stone were the worst. They treated everyone who wasn't one of them as a rock-ant, deserving to be crushed beneath a heel.

Regardless, the hour passed quickly—too quickly. Veronika's words remained in his mind, and right as the show was about to begin, Heath leaned forward and hugged Karo. "Remember, no matter what, we stay calm."

"You saying that for you, or for me?" His friend smirked.

"Probably both."

"Fair enough."

The lights beyond the stage went out. Darkness dominated the tent. Heath awaited Gerard's words, the words he'd heard almost every day for nearly half a decade.

"In the beginning, there was only light."

From the darkness of backstage, they watched a giant glowing orb of light appear in the center of the tent. Created by Gerard himself, the glow was a mere parlor trick, one of the few Talents the circus master could manage. Still, the chorus of awes from the crowd ensured people found it fantastic all the same.

"From light, sprang life. For the light was our Lord, and he was everything, but he wanted to be more than just everything. He wanted there to be life."

The orb shattered into a million pieces, starlight sprinkling toward the floor. Silk waves, rushed along tracks beneath the stage, whirled around Gerard's feet. "Across the Eternal Plane, the Lord scattered himself, seeding the world with a million million souls. But not all souls were created equal."

Hundreds upon hundreds of the lights shined more brightly than the rest, the lesser lights dimming and disappearing until only a couple dozen remained.

"Once, Gods walked among men," Gerard said, "until one-by-one, they died. Yet their descendants remained. Lived lives. Took their fragments and performed great feats of wonder. And as the power of our Lord wanes, the power of the Empire waxes."

A single light shone, eclipsing all others. It grew in size before dividing into six orbs, each spinning and vibrating until . . .

Darkness.

Then the light returned.

Standing on the stage were the firebreather brothers, two sword masters, and two animal tamers, all dressed in heroic garb. They flipped and whooped, dancing with one another in a flurried frenzy. Music trumpeted from beneath the stage, and their steps stampeded to the rhythm of the drums. Incense burned from braziers throughout the tent, infatuating the senses.

"Heroes of old, heroes of new, time is a construct we constantly undo." Gerard, having disappeared from view, amplified his voice. Another one of his talents. "Upon the founding of the Empire, six magnificent warriors protected us from the perils and evils of the world. Over the centuries, their souls have returned to us." The dance continued, but each warrior disappeared, one-by-one, leaping into the shadows backstage. "Yet as time fragmented them, their power faded."

One final warrior remained, played by Marcos, one of the animal handlers. He stood there, tall, an axe in one hand, a torchgem in the other.

"One hero's soul, Bastion the Omnipotent, has not been seen for generations. Neither fragment nor echo or queue song has found his sound and shared it with the world."

Marcos leapt from the stage. Heath climbed the ladder hidden by curtains, Karo right behind him. At the top, Heath found his trapeze swing ready and waiting. Karo shimmied along past, his station higher and further above the stage.

"Yet a prophecy speaks of a time when Bastion will return, his soul untarnished and unblemished."

The words were his signal. Heath descended, flying through the air above the crowd. Once the routine began, he always droned out Gerard's words. They interrupted his focus, and besides, Gerard always waited for queues from those in the air, rather than the other way around. And so zen arrived. Heath glided like he was swimming through water, floating between leaps and drifting between swings. The bars and ropes were his to command.

When Karo joined him in the air, near the end of the segment, they danced together as one, eyes meeting. They smiled. Heath winked. They jabbed at each other, but when in the moment of the show, they only knew one another. They were together, as they should be.

The show neared its zenith. Flames erupted. Heath looked down at the crowd for the first time—and found all eyes upon him.

Only him.

Their white masks stared upward, hiding their faces. It could be the Emperor. His wife. A princess. A duke. Anyone under those masks. But the red painted eyes stared at him, and only him.

He flipped. He shut out the thought. He landed. Karo dropping beside him.

"And when Bastion returns . . ." Gerard's voice boomed. "When Bastion returns, the Empire's End will arrive, only stopped by a pure and holy Bastion. For a demon will arrive too, ready to strike and smite and tempt Bastion to fall from glory."

Karo stepped forward, a red dagger in hand. The rubber toy slid into Heath's side, and together, they fell through the floorboards of the stage, landing in the net below.

* * *

The show continued. Battles between good and evil, fire and water, air and earth, they all played out. Heath and Karo executed their roles in other moments, soaring when needed, but there was never anything as thrilling as the first moments of the show. Just the two of them, revealing power through flight.

The show wound down. It ended. The lights all ignited, and from their little corner behind the stage, Heath watched the shadowy royal cabal stand in applause. Gerard and Alaiza stepped forward, bowing.

"Thank you, thank you, you honor us with your very presence," Gerard said. "Please, if there is anything else we can do for you tonight, we are at your disposal."

A man in a silvery cloak stepped forward. "Bring us the two boys."

A cough caught in Heath's throat, and he reflexively grabbed Karo's hand. "They're talking about us," he whispered. Was this what Veronika had been worrying about? Frantically, Heath looked for her, but she was probably outside, tending her monkeys. Any other opportunity for escape? But no.

Reggi grabbed their arms. "Come on friends."

"Heath, Karo, come meet our esteemed guests!" Alaiza's baritone boomed. As Reggi ushered them onto the stage, Alaiza leaned back and whispered, "Don't make a fool of us."

Heath half-smiled before turning toward the crowd. He knelt, motioning slightly with his left hand for Karo to follow suit. "Your worships, we are at your service."

The silvery man strode forward. Since they were up on the wooden stage, his mask was a few feet below. He gazed upward. From his cloak, he pulled a silver orb. Resting it in his left hand, he raised his right. Through black gloves, Heath noticed a slight glow. The man had a talent—what it did was another question entirely.

"From where do you both come?" the man asked.

"We were orphans in Panatamonia," Heath replied. "Since our tenth year, we've lived under the astute guidance of Alaiza and Gerard."

"Indeed." The man pocketed the orb. "And you." He pointed at Karo. "What are your dates of birth?"

"We were born the same day," Karo said, his voice level. "Our mothers were friends. They both died in childbirth."

"So sad." The man didn't sound sad. He paced back and forth, his mask tilting as if glancing between the two young men. After a moment, he turned around and faced the crowd of unknown onlookers. "These are the two." With a flourish, he pointed over his shoulder at Heath and Karo. "Orders?"

Heath had no way of knowing who the man was speaking to. And from what he could tell, the man received no verbal answer. Regardless, the silvery figure nodded as if he heard a response.

"Understood."

He twisted around with a flash of light, and silver spears left his palms. The bolts flew over Heath's head—he heard a gurgle. He tried to resist, but he glanced over his shoulder, discovering Alaiza and Gerard falling to their knees, gasping for breath. The silver spears were daggers now embedded in the circus masters' chests.

"I . . . thought we were . . . your servants," Gerard wheezed.

"And you have served us well," said their assailant. With his forefingers, he motioned toward Heath and Karo.

Out of the crowd, four more masked men in silver robes approached. As if gliding through darkness, the shadows leapt onto the platform and pulled rope from hidden pockets. Heath felt as if they should run. Flee. Do something. But his knees were frozen to the wood of the stage.

"Don't be afraid." The only member of the royal family to speak continued his monologue. "You both will be heading to safety with us. Simply *comply.*"

The final word felt touched with . . . more. Heath trusted this man. He was right. He would be heading to safety. The royal family couldn't possibly mean them harm.

"Karo, let them tie you up," Heath said.

"I agree," Karo replied. "I think we'll be just fine with them."

Their new friends gently placed the ropes around their wrists. They were tight, but Heath found the abrasive rope quite comfortable. With a lopsided smile, he stood and hopped off the stage. A dozen or so of the masked warriors suddenly held flame orbs in their hands, the physical manifestation of fire floating and glowing. They chucked the weapons toward the canvas. How nice of them to create a bonfire for the evening's festivities.

Heath and Karo followed their new friends out of the burning circus tent. Dozens of shadowy figures darted about the fairground, lobbing fireballs into the scattered wagons and cages and cabins. To Heath, it was all completely normal. There was no reason not to trust their friends. They simply needed to *comply.*

They passed through the makeshift gate, the shining pillars of Panatamonia in the distance. A series of carriages awaited them, white horses dutifully standing at ease. Their masked compatriots quickly ushered into the cabins of their transports, taking Karo and Heath toward separate cars.

"Wait," Heath said. *Comply.* He was complying. He simply had a question. "Why can't we ride together? We've never been separated."

"It's for your own safety," said their silvery protector. "You'll reunite when we reach the palace."

"That makes complete sense," Karo said. "It'll be fine!"

"Yes, it will be fine," Heath said.

Without any other comment, they moved into their separate carriages. Karo went with the men who bound them; Heath was joined by the speaker. Heath barely heard the screams coming from the circus behind them, and as the door to the carriage closed, all sound disappeared entirely. A few seconds later, the carriage began moving, the horses guiding them down the road and away from the bonfire forming at their backs.

The man removed his mask. They were alone in the carriage together, with light provided by a yellow glow-lamp embedded in its leather ceiling. In the dim ambiance, Heath saw a man maybe a few years older than Karo and him. Dark, disheveled hair, he was handsome in a subtle way. His brown eyes pierced the soul.

He stared at Heath for a long moment. Then, he said, "My name is Rikar. So Heath, do you have any talents you wish to share with me?"

"I'm talentless," Heath said. "I'm not anything special."

"That's not true," said the man. "You are quite special. You, and Karo, are part of the Prophecy. He is Bastion Reborn."

A fog slowly lifted from Heath's mind. His thoughts barely cleared. A voice deep inside yelled to RUN, yet another said *stay calm*. Rikar, sitting across the carriage, looked nice. He looked like someone he could trust. And then—

"Karo is Bastion Reborn?"

"Yes. Do you know what that makes you?"

Heath shook his head. He knew, but the answer wouldn't reach the tip of his tongue. He knew. Right?

"It makes you a demon. Specifically, *the* demon which, if not dealt with, will ensure the complete collapse of the Empire of Panatamonia. And we can't allow that to happen, now can we?"

Heath still felt happy. At the same time . . . he felt foreboding. Sweat dripped down his forehead. Was the carriage heating up?

Rikar twitched. "I thought you said you don't have any talents?"

"I don't, Mister Rikar," Heath said. "I just—"

The cabin exploded.

* * *

"By the divine souls, wake up!"

Heath wanted to die. His head throbbed. As consciousness awoke, he found echoing pain waiting for him—everywhere.

"I see your eyes fluttering . . ."

Ice stabbed his face, and with a shudder, he sat up, rubbing his eyes in an attempt to flush them.

Someone had thrown ice water on him.

"What? Where am I?" His vision cleared, though only slightly. A vague figure snapped a few fingers in front of his eyes.

"You're safe."

"Who are you?"

"You've had a concussion, I suspect."

Fog wrapped its way around his mind at the word, as if saying the comment revealed the truth of the throbbing pain racking his brain. "You—you didn't answer my question."

"It's me, Heath. Veronika."

"Nika? Where's Karo?"

"Probably in Panatamonia by now."

And with the mention of the capital, everything rushed back into Heath's memory. The performance before the royals. The attack on the circus. On their home. On their *family*. Then, they were whisked away by a strange man, and—separated.

"We have to save Karo!" he said, but the very effort of shouting the words sent a stab through his chest.

"No."

Veronika's features clarified. His vision focused. "No? What do you mean *no*?"

"I heard the words that Rikar fellow told you. And you don't know even close to half the truth yet. I don't know close to half the truth yet! Suffice to say, you and Karo are about to be the most wanted two individuals in the world."

"Rikar—he called me a demon. Am I a demon?"

"You are only what you choose to be," Veronika replied.

You are only what you choose to be. He didn't understand. He wanted to save Karo. He *needed* to save his friend. The only person he loved. He tried to rise again, but the pain—and Veronika's gentle push—kept him on the ground.

"Your carriage went a different direction than the rest of the cabal. That's how I managed to save you."

"Save me? How is this saving me?"

"Rikar was going to murder you."

Stunned silence filled the air, though Heath understood the magnitude of the scheme at hand. The circus, destroyed. Their capture. The flight. The masks. Everything orchestrated. Why, he didn't know, but it was as classic a setup as any from the legends. So wasn't he supposed to stand up, fly into town, and save his friend?

"It's not your moment to play hero yet," she said. "But that time will come. You've heard the same prophecy over and over again every night for years. Never did you think it was about you, did you? Well, it's not the only version of the prophecy. There are dozens. Hundreds." She sighed. "The Empire believes they know the *true* version of the prophecy. They might. But there's no way to know. And I'm here to tell you there's another path forward for you."

Heath shook his head. It was all too confusing. All too overwhelming.

"They think you're a demon," she said, as if not noticing his worry. "I think you're the hero of the story."

"This is ridiculous," he said. Without asking, she handed him a canteen of water. He took a sip. "It's impossible. We were just circus freaks, destined for a life on the road. We aren't the souls told of in legends of old."

"They believe Karo is," she said, "so if you want to save your friend, you must become what they believe you to be."

"A demon?"

"Only if you let them define you as such."

"Who the hell are you?" Heath couldn't help but smile, though. "Veronika, the monkey trainer? Or something else?"

"For now, something else. So make your choice. Will you join me? Will you follow me? Will you subvert their prophecy?"

All Heath wanted was to save Karo. Over Veronika's shoulder and far in the distance, he could see the gleaming lights of Panatamonia. Somewhere nearby, wood and stone and flesh burned—the circus. And in front of him, a young woman waited for an answer. For the first time, he noticed, at her feet, three of her flying monkeys waiting patiently.

"If the only way to save Karo is to follow you," he said, "Then I must follow."

"Good." She smiled. "Two circus souls are destined to save the world. Those are the words I know as truth. Let's make it so."

"I don't know about saving the world," Heath retorted. "Let's start with saving Karo."

"Good enough."

And so they settled into rest. Veronika fed him and tended his wounds. The monkeys kept guard. Heath didn't know what awaited him, but he understood what he must do if he was to save Karo from those masked fiends.

Absolutely anything.

He didn't care what prophecy said about Bastion. Or what the prophecy said about the demon who would follow in his wake.

Those were words written by old men.

He would tear everything down to save Karo from a fate without freedom.

Convergence

The mist faded from her eyes as she sat up from the stasis bed.

"Professor Smotters, welcome to Anvari," a musical voice said from her left. "We're very happy you have finally arrived."

Smotters. Was that her name? Ah, yes, Cyndi Smotters.

"Amnesia will wear off momentarily," said the voice. "We're happy to report the Recovery Module has successfully counteracted any long-term effects."

God, how she longed for the day when the Jump drives were stable enough for humans to travel at a rate four units faster than light. As it stood, trips to the nearest colonies took over two years, with the furthest taking five to seven. Still, the travel time was better than what the original colonists chose to endure at the beginning of the century. Oh how happy she was that such an ordeal had not been hers to bear.

The amnesia was annoying, though, even if only momentary.

Cyndi glanced up to see the source of the melodic noise. A human-imitating synth looked down, its facial construct creating a small smile. While many synths were designed to appear distinctly separate from humans, medical synths were an exception in order to provide an empathetic connection with patients.

"Thank you, friend," Cyndi said. "I would love to gather my belongings and meet my contact as soon as possible."

Her contact. How'd she know she had a contact? Like a bubble waiting to burst, her consciousness suddenly recalled the relevant information—but not all of it. There was beauty and pain in instantaneous communication. A few years ago, the colony on Anvari informed the ISA of their need for someone of Cyndi's talents. Thankfully, it was not an emergency situation. Anvari waited quite some time to have their request filled, even though Cyndi had accepted the position within a week of its appearance on the ISA boards. She waited another two months before the ISA gathered a full batch of colonists for Anvari.

"You'll be happy to know an apartment has already been prepared for you with your belongings so you may get ready in private. Also, you are the three-hundred-thousand-seven-hundred-forty-third person to arrive on Anvari."

Of the twenty-three extra solar colonies currently established, Anvari was one of the smaller ones, and it housed more people than had been in space just over a hundred years ago. It always astounded her how quickly the ISA had gotten the ball rolling.

"Thank you for the update," she said. "I would love for you to show me to that room."

Cyndi stood and followed the synth out of the awakening room and into a corridor of what she presumed was Anvari's spaceport. If she remembered her colonial history, there was a good chance the bulk of this building was actually the original colony ship. The hallway opened into a main forum, but before she could look around and really notice any of her surroundings, a well-dressed, white-haired pale woman approached Cyndi.

"Professor Smotters, I presume?" the woman inquired.

"Yes, correct," she said. Cyndi still failed to recall planet-side contact.

"Welcome to Anvari!" she said. "My name is Emali Richards, and I've been so excited for the day that you would arrive here."

Cyndi still drew a blank. "I am honored by that, Emali," she said cordially, trying to hide the confusion certainly slipping through her mannerisms.

"Of course, you'll want to get yourself settled before your work begins, but if you have time, you should come visit my organization," the woman said, holding out a business card. "I must continue on now!"

The overly friendly woman quickly moved onward, approaching another of the fresh arrivals. The entire time, the synth had stood by patiently waiting. "Shall we continue?" it said nonchalantly.

"Lead on."

With the strange woman heading off to badger someone else, Cyndi looked around the large enclosed space they were traversing. Various individuals milled about and sat waiting on benches. A vast glass wall allowed natural light into the building. Most likely, the building doubled as a sort of airport. Various screens lit up with the few flights ready to transport citizens to the other towns on this planet.

What caught Cyndi's attention was the sight beyond the wall of windows. At the base of the transparent wall waited a long set of doors. Beyond, various clusters of residential and commercial modules stood tall and vibrant, transported directly from manufacturing orbitals surrounding Earth.

The more impressive architectural feats were the buildings not from Sol. The population of Anvari had moved beyond the colony modules and constructed various sleek, low-lying buildings around what she assumed was the center of town. Of course, solar panels and wind turbines protruding from roofs powered the buildings completely.

The city was a sustainable paradise.

The city's planners had artistically placed natural fauna along the paths and central areas of the town. One detail amazed her more than any other, though.

There were no roads.

Nor cars.

Or vehicles of any type at all.

Bicycles moved about throughout the town. Indeed, Cyndi was certain the only powered transportation on the planet lived in the building she was about to leave. She had heard of the alternative infrastructure styles developed on the colony worlds, but she had not realized the truly revolutionary approach undertaken. Earth, long ago, decided sustainability took form through electric cars, mass transportation, and technologically-advanced infrastructure. But those advancements had been a necessity, given the way civilizations had progressed over thousands of years. When provided a new start, Cyndi was glad that some humans chose refreshing alternatives.

She inhaled in the stale air of the airport, her last taste of her old life. A few seconds later, the synth led Cyndi through the doors. She breathed again. The air of Anvari was sweet. Fresh. Unlike any place she'd ever experienced.

They walked down a street. Well, what amounted for a street here, since it was completely pedestrian. The path inclined slightly up a hill away from the transportation hub. Well-trimmed shrubs and trees lined the walkway—she didn't recognize the species, but they reminded her of the bushes and trees outside any building back home. Others, most likely native based on the blueish tinge to their leaves, dotted other pathways crisscrossing between the living modules. She found all of it fantastic and beautiful—and eerily familiar.

"I realized I haven't asked your name," Cyndi said, glancing at the synthetic. "I am so sorry, I've just been so focused on taking everything in."

"No need for apologies," it said. "I like to call myself Sela."

"How long have you been here?" Cyndi asked as they walked.

Sela waited to answer as they approached a living complex. The SI opened a door without touching it, using what Cyndi assumed was digital recognition software. "I was built in the year 2154. I arrived on Anvari in 2170, and have been here for seven years. Translated into standard time, I have been here for fifteen years."

"How has your life on this planet been?"

Sela tilted its head at Cyndi in a quizzical fashion. "I'm not sure what you mean by that question."

Cyndi had forgotten not all synths had abstract reasoning capabilities. It was incredibly difficult to tell the difference between the actually conscious and the simple "service" androids.

"Never mind," she said. They walked up a set of stairs.

Sela approached a white door with an ornately carved 3C embedded into the metal. Cyndi chuckled quietly. Some things never change.

"Is something humorous?" Sela said.

"Eh, not really," she said. "It's just that 3C was my apartment number back where I lived on Earth."

"That is quite a coincidence," Sela said.

Not even a laugh. She thought most synth service bots had humor programs. Sela certainly was not self-aware, but perhaps its humor settings couldn't detect coincidental comedy.

"I cannot access your room," Sela said. "This is where I bid you farewell and return to my post."

"I thank you for your kindness, Sela."

The synth nodded and walked back toward the stairs.

The door was locked by fingerprint. Cyndi placed her palm on the pad beside the door. With a soft click, the door slid upwards.

The room was not large, containing a bed, bathroom, one table, and a small kitchen unit, but it was exactly what Cyndi requested. A set of clothes waited on her bed, and her personal digital notebook was sitting on the table. She had always preferred notebooks over the enhanced reality offered by other tech. She doubted citizens here had augmented much of their reality with any underlying digital framework yet, anyways.

On one of the walls, she noticed a thin, clear video screen lighting up with the words, "message waiting." Walking up to the monitor, she pressed "receive," then proceeded to listen to the message as she changed out of the outfit she had been wearing for way too long.

"Hello Dr. Smotters, my name is Ian Heart," the voice said. "We spoke briefly before your flight left, and it's been a long wait for us on this end, though I am sure it was quite short for you."

Ian Heart. Her contact's name. Finally, she remembered.

The outfit they had laid out for her was . . . exotic. That was the word. Tight-fitting, but modest at the same time. And comfortable. And an incredibly breathable material.

". . . I'm sure you're getting yourself acquainted to your new home, but as soon as you have a chance, come down to the lab. We've been aching to introduce you to your work. Your notebook will have received the directions."

Cyndi opened the cooler. Inside, she found a bowl of sliced fruit. Placing it on the counter, she looked at the strange food with furtive curiosity. Taking a slice in hand, she analyzed the texture and colors as well as the scent. It looked like an apple, yet it had the aroma of an orange. Intrigued, she took a bite. It tasted like an apple too.

"At your convenience, stop by the town center in the middle of the green. The people there will help you get acquainted with Anvari, your new home. I hope to be working with you soon."

The message chimed, signifying completion. Taking a seat at the table to finish the strangely familiar fruit, Cyndi powered up her notebook. The first thing to show up were her missed messages—hundreds of them. She quickly sorted by sender, and searched for those from her family. There were dozens. She hesitated, knowing the life events she would have missed, like Luci's graduation. "I'll look at those after meeting with Ian," she said aloud to herself. Right now she did not feel like dealing with emotions, especially because she couldn't completely place memories to the feelings yet. Too many thoughts were still slowly coming back to her. Besides, it was not as if she left without telling anyone. They had a two-month notice. They knew she'd be gone for those events. For everything, for the foreseeable future.

She continued to browse her mail for messages from the University of London. They were asking her to be a long-distance video professor—intriguing. Another listed her latest paper as being published on her behalf, just six months ago.

So much was left behind, but for what? She really needed to go find out, since her memory was failing to remind her of the details. Placing her notebook in the bag on the table after memorizing the directions to the lab, she took one last slice of the strange fruit. She put the bowl back in the cooler and headed out the door, messenger bag wrapped over her shoulder.

* * *

The lab was not difficult to find, sitting on the edge of town down the street from her new home. Finding it was the easy part. Getting inside, on the other hand, looked like it might be a chore.

Outside the structure, protesters stood with a variety of signs and posters in an assortment of colors. Many of the signs had phrases relating to the brutality of animal experimentation. Others had something to do with the sanctity of life—and the respect due the forerunners. Whatever that meant.

As Cyndi approached the crowd, a man turned toward her. "Have you come to join us in our boycott of the heretics?" he asked. "We can't let them break the union we have created with this planet!"

"Not exactly," Cyndi said, walking past the man. The crowd was no more than fifty strong, stopping at the white stone steps leading up to the lab. The lab itself matched the sleek archways and curved roofs she'd noticed as indicative of Anvari's own architecture. Standing on the steps, three men waited, lazily leaning against marble pillars. Security, she presumed, though they didn't look particularly concerned or threatened by the protest. Their relaxed demeanor signaled they took no side—most likely present to ensure safety for all.

Cyndi slowly made her way through the crowd, listening to the words of those around her as she shuffled people out of the way. She understood less than half of what they were saying, but what she could understand sounded like typical fringe anti-intellectual sentiment. Strange. She wouldn't have expected such ideals to make their way to one of the colonies. Most of those types loathed the outward expansion of the human species.

At the front of the crowd, she spotted the woman from earlier. Not wanting to make a scene, Cyndi attempted to slip by unnoticed, but the dice failed to roll in her favor.

"You found us quite quickly!" Emali exclaimed. "I am quite pleased. Even new colonists know what's best for our sister, Anvari."

Cyndi was now completely lost. "I'm sorry, but I am not here for the protest," she said. She tried to choose her words carefully. "I'm just exploring town."

Emali looked unconvinced, making her smile all the more disconcerting. "That certainly is your right. There is nothing good for you in this building, however."

Cyndi brushed her off and walked up the stairs. She could not shake the feeling she was supposed to know more about that woman. No matter. It was time to focus on what was before her. The protesters started directing their yells toward Cyndi, and the officers at the top of the steps gave her a disconcerting look. She hoped the protest would not transform into a riot.

One of the peace officers signaled for her to stop. "No admittance without clearance. I've definitely never let you in here before, so unless you happen to be the new director, you should head home."

"Well, supposedly I'm the new director," she said, a bit annoyed the officers hadn't been briefed on her identity. "How do I get clearance?"

The man pulled out a handprint scanner. "You either have clearance or you don't. Hand please."

She pressed her hand against the scanner. It glowed green with confirmation.

"My apologies, Doctor Smotters. They were hoping you would stop by today, but I thought it likely you would want a day to collect yourself here on this new world."

"How long has"—she nodded slightly toward the crowd—"this been going on?"

"Ever since the new lab opened a month ago. They mostly ignored the old lab, but it was pretty far outside of town."

Cyndi looked at the badge on his chest. "Thank you, Bridges."

He smiled. "My pleasure. Stay safe, and leave the building when everyone else does."

He let her pass, and the volume of jeers directed toward her nearly doubled. She heard varied insults, ranging from naming her the whore of the devil to a hater of harmony. What was with these people?

As she approached the door, it slid open, revealing a man waiting for her. "Dr. Smotters?" he said, holding out his hand. "I'm Ian Heart. Let's get inside so we can talk in peace."

She shook his hand and followed him inside the lab. The doors closed, muffling the protest enough so that it was no longer audible. The noise was still there, however, in the background. Through the doors they walked into a small lobby or common area of sorts. A synth sat at a desk. A young woman lounged on a couch, eating a sandwich. Two hallways split from the room heading in two directions; a sign over the left hallway said *Organism Storage*; the sign over the right read *Genetics Lab*.

Ian led her to the couch where the young woman was eating. "Dr. Smotters, meet Miri Kennington. She will be your technician. I handle the organisms and specimens. And you . . . well, we're glad to finally have a xenobiologist on Anvari again."

Miri finished her bite then smiled from ear to ear. "We're so glad you're finally here. We can't say it enough. Maybe we can finally prove those bastards outside wrong."

"Miri!" Ian said.

Cyndi chuckled. "Those bastards outside? I simply can't figure out what's going on here. Besides the strange anti-science behavior outside, you said 'have a xenobiologist again.' What happened to the old one?"

Miri's smile faded, and she pointed outside. "You don't remember the news bulletin attached with the job posting, do you? Amnesia must still be hitting you. Well, that happened." She waved a hand toward the entrance.

"You mean the protests scared them away or something?"

Ian cracked his knuckles. "No. Our old xenobiologist is the heart of the Harmonic Church of Anvari. She founded it. You might have met her, she loves introducing herself to new arrivals. Emali?"

Realization dawned as memory of the news bulletin arose in Cyndi's mind. Something about an esteemed scientist sabotaging an entire lab and completely abandoning her team in the middle of a forest. "I see. What happened?"

Miri made her hands look like her brain was exploding. "She went wacko. Bonkers. Bat shit crazy."

Ian gave Miri another look. "Emali was one of the original colonists.

Her experiences those first few years researching the wildlife here really shaped her outlook on the planet. Five years ago, when we discovered something . . . well, we'll show you what we discovered in a bit. But what we discovered sent her off the deep end."

"Should I be worried about safety?"

"Bridges outside seems to think so, but as of now, the church hasn't done anything violent. It's only really gained any real influence over the past year or so."

Miri nodded in agreement. "In other news, did you hear your last article was published?"

"Miri is kind of a big fan of your work," Ian said.

"How can I not be, given she was the first biologist to actually spend time writing about the implications of the genetic material found on Anvari?" her cheeks turned bright red, though.

"Speaking of your work, would you like to see what we're analyzing?" Ian asked.

Cyndi said, "Certainly, but what about that 'big' discovery?"

"That is the 'big' discovery. So hold on. Suspense can be a good thing sometimes."

The three headed down the hallway toward Organism Storage.

"The first few creatures we pulled DNA from were plants, as well as some lizard-like creatures we found throughout the forests," Ian said. "This planet also has an animal 'kingdom' analog to bugs on Earth—Emali named them Caloids. She thought they looked like bugs she had seen growing up in California."

"What bugs live in California that don't live elsewhere?" Cyndi said.

"We told you she was batty," Miri said.

"Some of the similarities were striking," Ian said as he opened the door to the final room. "But then we found this little guy."

The room was filled with various plants and small organisms all in various habitat enclosures. In the middle of the room, an enclosure bigger than the others spread outward. A small furry creature sat licking its paw. At first, Cyndi thought her eyes were being deceived. Sitting before her was a cat. Not a domesticated cat, for sure, but a wild cat the size of a house cat. It had similar eyes, color patterns, and proportions. If it was thrown in the wild on Earth, it would blend right in.

"Whiskers here is what caused Emali to quit everything."

"I can't say I understand why," Cyndi said. "A conundrum like this is a scientist's dream come true."

"She didn't see it that way," Miri said. "She refused to even look at the data."

"I'm assuming it has unique bases, correct?" Cyndi asked.

"Of course," Ian said. "But Emali's church is claiming some crazy mythological explanation about ancient aliens seeding this world and Earth with life. It's a sign toward how to transcend existence, or some other gibberish that I ignore."

"What?" Cyndi said, genuinely baffled.

"Bat shit crazy . . ." Miri said under her breath.

"Whiskers, for all obvious phenotypic purposes, is a cat," Ian said. "We've found others of her species, out in the forests north of Lynsberg. Besides the need for a qualified biologist to assist in the continual catalog of the species of Anvari, we need someone like you to explore Whiskers's species."

Cyndi put her hand up to her hair, running her fingers straight along her scalp. "Does anyone on Earth know about Whiskers?"

"Not yet," Ian said. "Emali knows obviously, but she has actually hid the existence of the creature from her followers, for now. She probably fears they would start asking too many questions, though in reality it would probably give her more power. She may be saving it as a big reveal, who knows. Which is why we need to get a statement out quickly. Fortunately, the creatures live far enough away from Lynsberg that we only discover them on deep field expeditions." The three of them headed back toward the lobby.

"We don't want to send any data back before we have a reasonable explanation to give," Miri said. "We don't want to start some crazy church back on Earth, too."

Given their experience here, Cyndi agreed. It was a valid concern. She could not fathom what these two must have gone through over the past few years. She gained respect for their passion and resilience every minute she spent with them. Working under the watchful eye of a cult was never easy.

"Tell me, have you found any other creatures similar to this one when compared to a specimen back on Earth?" she asked.

"We have," Ian said. "Nothing really matches anything on Earth exactly, but a few are very similar to mice—except they lay eggs."

Cyndi sat in contemplation for a moment before glancing out one of the tinted windows toward the protestors. Some things never change.

"I think the answer," she said, "lies obviously on our doorstep."

Both Miri and Ian looked at her, tilting their heads in confusion.

"On Earth, strange cult movements show up everywhere, all the time, in very strange and different settings, but they almost always have a similar structure. Fanatical leaders, strange beliefs, etcetera. Likewise, in biology, we've seen similar structures evolve separately in different locations. Eyes, for example. Also, on each planet we've discovered that has rudimentary organisms, there is always some sort of analog for plants. Chloroplasts apparently are very easily naturally selected. Are you guys following?"

They both nodded their heads.

"On Anvari, and many of the colony worlds, we're seeing new forms of DNA. New bases. However, it just so happens that the phenotype of a cat was a very survivable phenotype in this planet's environment. By sheer coincidence, we have discovered a key example of convergent evolution. Sure, we're probably going to find some differences in this cat from Earth cats . . . but likewise, cults always have different beliefs. They always end up being the same in the end, however."

"What, bat shit crazy?" Miri said.

* * *

Cyndi lounged on her bed and kicked off her shoes. After a long day completing lab paperwork and filing it with the various funding institutions back on Earth, she walked back to her apartment. Ian and Miri invited her out for drinks at a local bar—apparently a distillery made a fancy whiskey from a native grain—but she politely declined.

She was tired.

And confused.

How could a scientist like Emali Richards fall toward conspiracy? Cyndi had said her words back at the lab—and she tended to agree with Miri. It was all bat shit crazy. But saying those words didn't *explain* why the scientist shifted easily toward conspiracy and the formation of a religious cult. What drove her to madness?

Between filing papers and chatting with Ian and Miri, Cyndi read Emali's earliest field reports. She was a meticulous scientist, detailed and precise in her xenobiology. Her observations were insightful and perceptive. She didn't read like a woman who would suddenly shift into the form of a zealot.

Yet there she was, leading a cult.

Leaning over to the small bedside table, Cyndi retrieved her digital notebook. She took a few minutes to snap a few messages back to friends and family on Earth, so they all knew she arrived safely on Anvari. Some point soon, she'd need to schedule a quantum call with her mothers to check-in.

Just as she clicked send on a note to a cousin, a knock echoed on the door.

Cyndi slid off the bed and tiptoed toward the entrance to her apartment. As she approached, a screen on the door materialized, revealing a woman wearing all black standing on the other side—Emali. Waiting beneath a glowing LED, her dark visage looked ominous.

Yet this was Anvari, shining jewel of the frontier worlds. Cyndi didn't have a reason to fear for her life.

Right?

She triggered the command for the door to slide open. "Hello?"

"Dr. Smotters, is this a bad time?" said Emali.

Cyndi glanced out the hall toward the dark sky, where two moons shone brightly in orbit. "No, not at all." She motioned toward the table a few feet inside the door. "Feel free to come in."

Emali passed the threshold, and as they both settled at the table, the door slid shut.

"Frankly," Cyndi said, "I'm surprised to see you here."

"I'm sure Ian and Miri have 'briefed' you on everything you need to know about me," the older scientist said. From her coat, she pulled a folder filled with documents—paper, not plastic. "I'm giving you these files just so you can understand everything you need to know about me. I'm not a monster. I know they'll try to say I'm a monster. I'm not."

The papers lingered on the table between them. "I don't think you're a monster," Cyndi said, "but I am confused."

Emali smirked. "Of course you're confused. You've now seen what I've seen. You're trying to figure out why I now lead a cult. You think I'm crazy. You think I'm mad. You think this world deserves better. Maybe some or all of those thoughts are true. Am I right?"

"Possibly."

"I'll just need you to read those documents. But after I leave."

"I'm unconvinced." Cyndi leaned back in her chair. "You accost me five seconds after I arrive, you protest my new place of work, and now you show up at my doorstep. I'm the woman who's taken your old position, what could you possibly want from socializing with me?"

"For the two of us to come to an understanding." From her pocket, Emali pulled a leather piece of tan jerky, tearing into it with her teeth. After chewing and swallowing, she returned the dried meat to her coat. "We're going to see a lot of one another over the next few months and years. I simply want to ensure we understand one another."

"You betrayed all your science and ideals to run a crazy religious cult!"

Emali stood, pushed in her chair, and headed toward the door. "Just read the documents." The door slid open as she approached—most likely recognizing her as a leaving visitor. Cyndi was alone in her room once more.

For the next hour, she left the folder sitting on the table as she attempted to sleep. But it was a restless sleep. She tossed, rolled around, failed to find a comfortable spot with the strangely silky pillows. As her clock read 1am—whatever that meant given Anvari's nonstandard rotation—she slipped out of bed again and returned to the table. Opening the folder, her jaw dropped. She rushed to the cabinet, found a glass, and filled it with water. Sitting down, she settled in to read.

Acceptance of Grant Request

To: Emali Richards
Date: February 2, 2172
Subject: Sociological/Anthropological Proposal

Dr. Richards,

This note confirms our receipt and acceptance of your research proposal to study the impacts of cult interactions on a young colony world, particularly a colony with unique biological features ripe for use in religious experience. As you outlined in your proposal, a hands-on approach will be necessary to ensure the cult is properly guided and observed from within. To that end, we are prepared to fund your work for 1 million USD each year, with grant reports quarterly on the progress of your work. We look forward to your observations; the methodology you have proposed is sound.

Best regards,

The Mars Institute Research Review Board
Attachment Enclosed

To Mars—and Love

Elizabeth pushed her lunch around the plate as she listened to her friends go on and on about the daily gossip. They were like birds singing during an early spring day. *Boring.* Though she participated occasionally. Gossip was usually harmless, but often it left a vile taste in her mouth afterward.

"Did you guys hear?" Clair said. The spittle was almost visible as she took no time at all to annunciate her words. "Kit is supposedly holding a party this weekend!"

"Tricia told me about it yesterday," Jennifer said, "She's got her older brother hooking Kit up with the drinks."

"I'm sure it'll be totes fabulous," Clair said. "I hope Kit invites plenty of the football team. Their last match against that Club from Oxford will make some great conversation to move things in a more interesting direction."

Elizabeth mentally rolled her eyes. It was always boys with Clair. Never anything else. They were in their final years of secondary school before going to university, and still, all Clair cared about was boys. Elizabeth found boys interesting. She just did not find them to be a subject worth discussing constantly with every friend or breathing organism in the immediate vicinity. Elizabeth indulged Clair as one indulges a child, though, since she had known her for too long. It was something trivial, nothing worth getting truly annoyed over.

Bored, Elizabeth decided to pull up her unread messages on her retinal Lens. With a subtle mental command, her field of vision was flooded with a variety of different options. Selecting emails took a simple thought-push, and two unread notes appeared. Ignoring the first as spam, Elizabeth opened the second from a forum friend.

"You still up for tonight?" the message said—from StarGazerAstral.

Quickly, she prepared a response in her mind and submitted it. "For sure! I'll see you server side at 1800!" She ended it with a smiley face. The message was sent successfully—from EmpiricalGirl2048. Hearing her name—her real name—promptly brought Elizabeth back to the real world.

"What?" she said, not having heard the question.

"Were you dreaming again?" Clair asked.

"No, I was just online for a second," Elizabeth said. "What's up?"

"I am still majorly jealous you already have one of those things installed." Jennifer said. "That 'eighteen years' requirement is so annoying!" Elizabeth held back stating the obvious reason for why the age limit was in place.

"Anyways, we were wondering what you thought of that dork William's decision to go to school over in America. I think he was definitely just running away from everything that happened last year. Seriously, can people not take jokes?"

Elizabeth really wanted to ignore the question, but everyone was looking at her. Last year, the general population of the school bullied William Rickard, a bright kid in their grade. Subsequently, he graduated early to study math at MIT across the pond in Boston.

She'd liked him. He was smart. They got along in their classes. But the chances of ever seeing him again were like her chances of actually getting the living stipend for Cambridge. It always made her want to vomit when she remembered how her friends had instigated most of the bullying. They certainly would not understand why she liked him.

"I say the best of luck to him," Elizabeth said. "MIT is an impressive school."

"Not as impressive as your acceptance to Oxford," Jennifer said.

It always amazed Elizabeth how they mocked William for the exact attributes her friends respected in her. So illogical.

"That's debatable," Elizabeth said, "but I appreciate the thought. Anyways, I'm still not sure between Oxford or Cambridge."

"At least you no longer have any competition," Clair said. "You'll give a fabulous speech at graduation."

"Let's hope so," Elizabeth said.

* * *

Elizabeth had little to say to her family as they finished eating the fish prepared by her father. They all knew what she was planning to watch tonight; she had been planning for months, and they asked no questions as she sped from the table and retired to her family's Connection Lounge. Sitting down in the Virtual chair, she brought up the Lens's menu once more. A new option appeared, showing her body's receptivity to enter Virtual.

Ever since she received the implants about three months ago, she tried to take some time a few days each week to enter the many available worlds. It was an exhilarating and simultaneously frightening experience. Today, however, was not experimental or for playing some game. Today, she had a date with a friend from some foreign land to meet together and witness history. More importantly, it would be brilliant fun to finally assign a face to the person she had been messaging on the forums after all this time. She knew the person could put up a façade if they wished, but she genuinely hoped they would keep their promise.

She certainly intended to. All walls down.

Elizabeth inputted in the unique server-hash, and two seconds later, she was whisked along a tunnel of blue-purple light. Her external sensations abruptly dimmed to almost nonexistent; conscious control over her limbs receded. She compared the experience to entering a daydream, yet without the awareness of the external world still present. Her vision of her family's house blackened, merging with the swirling lights.

A whole new world replaced her vision.

It was her private home within Hemisphere, the second-life world her parents' Virtual subscription included. She was lounging in a chair, surrounded by hundreds of books that were not actually all there. Through this library, she could access practically any book ever written. The house itself overlooked a gorge in a region known as Reinland. It was an expansive area with plenty of room and lots of hiking trails. 'Hemisphere' was a fictional world; the vistas created by the server's AI were eerily familiar to famous geographic locations on Earth. Some vistas even blew real world counterparts out of the water in their majesty. Elizabeth used it as a place to be able to go outside when desired if the weather outside of Virtual was inhospitable. Since she lived in England, that was pretty much every other day.

She had two bedrooms, though she doubted sleep would ever happen here. She really hoped she never became one of those people who spent more time in Virtual than in the real world. Besides the bedrooms, there was a sleek, industrial kitchen and an open aired entertainment room with a variety of couches and a fancy video screen. Going to her kitchen, Elizabeth ordered some ingredients from the fridge's display. Opening the door, she found avocados, limes, tomatoes, and all the other necessary ingredients to make fresh guacamole. While she could have just ordered the guacamole, that took all the fun out of tasting fresh guacamole through Virtual's sensory replicators.

By the time she was finishing placing the chips and guac in front of the television, it had almost reached 20:00. Sitting down on the couch, she said, "Video, Power On, and Access Public Access Research Broadcast Network."

The screen promptly revealed the channel requested. The volume was at the perfect level, adapted to her auditory systems. On the screen appeared a science reporter standing in front of a virtual display of one of the orbital platforms hundreds upon hundreds of kilometers above her real head. She doubted they had created a virtual analog in Hemisphere.

As she began to relax, the bell at her front door rang, sounding throughout the house. "You have a visitor," a loud electronic voice stated.

"I'll be right there," she yelled, bounding up from her spot to head toward the door. On her way down the front hall, she stopped to check herself in the mirror, noticing her messy hair. She went to use her hands, but then remembered where she was. Pulling up a quick mental menu as she walked, she set her hair to self-adjusting. No need to worry about her hair tonight.

"It doesn't need to be anything special," she thought to herself. "It's not as if you're trying to seduce them."

Slowly, Elizabeth opened the door to see the face of StarGazerAstral.

"Hi, my name is Will—" He abruptly paused. "William."

Elizabeth stared in disbelief, her mouth hanging wide open. William Rickard was StarGazerAstral? Of all the people in the world—well, the Virtual world—to be standing before her, why did it have to be him? He knew who her friends were. He knew how many times she had stood there and said absolutely nothing.

After a painfully silent moment, he said, "I should go."

Elizabeth realized her mouth was still hanging wide open. That probably wasn't making the situation any better. She closed it with haste. "No, William, wait," she said, adding a small amount of plea to her tone. "Please stay."

"Why?" he asked. "Do you have the rest of your little gang waiting in there with you? Are you guys trying to have the last laugh?"

"No, I promise, it's just me. I never wanted to hurt you last year, or the years before that. I never once said anything to you; it was all Clair and Jennifer. And I know that doesn't justify my inaction to try to stop them, but what am I supposed to do? Just turn my back on friends of ten years?"

"I used to hold you in such high respect, you know," William said. "Those anti-bullying speeches you made back in Grade Eight were so well written. But when your friends started playing the part, you played yours perfectly as well. The sideline bully is sometimes the most painful, you know."

"Yeah, well, you think I liked the consequences, seeing you disappear? I can't help who I am. I'm shy and introverted. I mentally curled up in a ball every time I wanted to be brave and stand up to my friends."

"Oh please," he said with disgust, "don't deny that you're happy I graduated early. Now you get to be number one."

Elizabeth was trying to hold back tears, but a few drifted down her cheeks. "For how smart you are, you can be a real ass sometimes. You've seen my writings online. You know my views on selfish action."

"What about selfish inaction? You're probably just as hypocritical regarding that."

"You still don't get it!" Elizabeth said vehemently. "I've worshipped your intellect since we first started classes together. You've always been one step ahead in everything, and I both hated and loved you simultaneously. I hated the fact that you would always be better than me. But I also loved the fact that I could always try to beat you. And then my friends chased you away, and I no longer had someone to chase."

"But—"

"I'm still not finished!" she said. "There was more than just competition between us. I came to love our banter within class, and I almost cried when that withered last year as my friends turned into witches. And when I learned you had graduated early, I was distraught I . . ." she trailed off.

"What?" he said. The anger faded from his eyes.

Elizabeth looked at him, tears welling in her eyes. William was stronger than ever yet still somehow broken. No matter what, he was the same person she had always admired, and she had come to similarly adore the online persona she had conversed with over the past months even more so. There were too many things she wished she could do. In some versions of this moment, dreamed over and over in her head, the conversation ended with a kiss, but she couldn't work up the courage to make that move. *Could she?* No. "I wish—I wish . . . No. You know what? There's nothing I can do to make up for what I've done. What I've failed to do. No more excuses. I was wrong. I need to perpetually own that I was wrong. That doesn't make up for the harm that occurred to you, but I can own that I was wrong. And I can invite you inside. No—I can do more than that. I can invite you back into my life. My real life. When will you be back in town? We're getting tea."

William leaned against the door frame, staring past her toward the screen showing the reporter rattling on and on about the upcoming test. "We're going to miss it," he said, "if we keep arguing."

Elizabeth glanced over her shoulder. "We can press rewind. This is more important."

He smiled—it was that smile she recognized from Calculus, when he knew his answer was right and someone else's was wrong.

"You know," he said, "I always had a lot of respect for you. I don't necessarily believe you yet, but . . . I'm willing to let you try to make me believe you."

She held out her hand. "That's all I ask. Let's start new. Let's watch what we planned to watch."

Furtively, he reached out and laced the digital representation of his fingers through her own. She led him inside, the door closing behind them. They plopped on the couch right as the reporter stopped speaking.

From their Virtual location, William and Elizabeth watched the feed of a camera placed atop a small vessel in orbit. Its drive activated. The space around the ship distorted, warping and crackling like a frying egg. Light danced like fireworks. Then—nothing. Well, not nothing. Something. The spacecraft's camera revealed a dance of black and white, light and dark, and a million unfathomable colors. They sat there, entranced, as the light show drew them into an unseen world of beauty and mystery.

Then, a few minutes later, the show stopped.

The ship, having once lived in orbit above Earth—the blue marble—rested above the Red Planet.

William and Elizabeth glanced at one another. From the look in his eyes, she could tell their fight was practically forgotten. "The implications!" he shouted.

"It's incredible," Elizabeth said. She stood, pulling a digital chalkboard out of thin air before them. "It's the Alcubierre theory, right?"

"I think so." He brandished a piece of chalk. "Incredible is the right word. But you know what this means, yeah? We've cracked interstellar space. People like you and me, we're going to be the pioneers. We're just the right age to chart a course for completely new worlds. We're it. We're going to Mars and beyond."

"To Mars," Elizabeth whispered. "And perhaps we can go to one of these distant worlds together." She said those words a little bit louder.

He glanced at her. "Yes, perhaps."

She smiled. "But first, we have a few wounds to heal here on Earth."

* * *

The next day, Elizabeth once again sat at the lunch table with her friends discussing the same old gossip. Their tongues flitted about like flies trying to escape a spider web. Their words were many, but their subject matter was nonsensical.

For once, however, Elizabeth started a conversation herself. "I heard William Rickard is coming home this weekend on his fall break and will be at Kit's party."

"What," Clair said. "Who invited that loser?"

"I did," Elizabeth said.

Patterns of Piracy

Emerald Jewel. The pride of the ICH, the planet more perfect than Earth itself. Billions lived on its surface. Many of their ancestors fled Earth's archaic ways to find a new life, a new world, a new hope for the future.

That's what everyone said, at least. Raith hated the planet. It was too green. Way too green. Whoever named it Emerald Jewel was playing a sick joke on everyone, describing it literally. The planet was practically a continuous lush forest, with almost no arid regions except near the poles where everything simply froze. From its beaches to its mountain vistas, Emerald Jewel stank of the opulence of the wealthy and opportunistic.

For where the wealthy congregated, humans—and SIs, like Raith—made their mark. It was way too easy to take advantage of the unwitting, unsuspecting, naïve tower-dwellers.

Hence Raith's present predicament. He was hanging from a carbon-steel wire from one of the tallest towers in Emerald City, slowly laser-cutting his way into rich person #5,274's apartment. Who they were, he didn't care, because they had exactly what he wanted. What he needed, actually.

"Three minutes," Roark said over the comm. "You've got three minutes before the tower's power cycle resets security."

"I'll be out in two, don't you worry," Raith replied.

A few seconds later, the laser completed its rotation. Using a suction from his tool belt, Raith controlled the fall of the glass, gently pushing it inward and gently letting it fall to the carpet below.

"I'm in." Raith pushed off the wall with his feet, narrowed his body, and slipped through the hole. The cable remained attached to the hook on his back to ensure a speedy retreat. "Apartment matches our blueprints." He crouched, furtively waddled toward a door on the left, and slowly opened it. The room—empty. As planned.

He entered the second room, cable quietly bouncing against the door.

Inside, he found a wooden desk—was that mahogany? On it waited a server, its light blinking blue. Raith approached, and, using AR, he pulled up its digital access point. The scripts provided by their employer worked immediately, and he was in, discovering files upon files. Financial data. Bank account access. Mercantile logs, including—there it was. Transit paths of valuable Exo shipments heading in and out of the system. Oh, and a bonus—the codes to rich person #6,743's personal racing pinnace. What a prize!

Without pause, Raith downloaded everything onto a partitioned Virtual drive. The upload speed of his body's personal network grabbed it all within a few seconds. He'd been inside the apartment for merely a minute.

"Ninety seconds," Roark said a moment later.

"I'm almost done," Raith replied. "Let me see . . ." He glanced at a shelf on the far wall. The apartment owner owned paper books. Rare things, they were. Most likely imported from Earth. He approached the bookshelf. It was filled with all manner of stories, but mostly classics from two or three centuries prior. And they all contained a similar theme—piracy, on the high seas. Curious. Raith snagged one title—*Deathly Shores*—and thumbed through its pages. He didn't know the last time he held a paperback—or why he would have held it. This man truly was rich. Too rich.

A sudden snip came from the other room. The cable slackened.

"Shit," he said privately through the comm. "I'm compromised. Wasn't this place supposed to be unoccupied tonight? Anyway, I need an alternate escape route." Without hesitating, Raith barreled through the office door, slamming a man right into the carpet. His quarry went sprawling. Raith rose swiftly from atop the battered door, pausing only long enough to get a good look at his unfortunate victim. The man was old—revealed by his pasty, wrinkly skin—but he had a muscled persona. Like he used to be a soldier.

Not good.

The man started rising, but Raith didn't wait. He sprinted away from the window. The cable now hung beyond the glass, out of reach or use.

"All right, I've got a path for you." Roark's voice sounded exhausted, as if he was breathing hard on behalf of Raith.

"Roger, send it along." Raith blasted through a door into the floor's main foyer. With the building's power out, red security lights flickered in the darkness. "What's my destination?"

"There's a private hangar two floors above you."

Of course. The codes to the racing pinnace he found. Why *wouldn't* the old man house his private racer inside the same building? If he didn't need to hotwire anything, he'd save plenty of time. Raith bounded for the stairs.

A shot rang over his shoulder. "Get back here, you damn tinny!"

Raith darted around the corner, kicked open a door, and leapt up the stairs. As the door closed, shots echoed off metal walls. Two at a time, he sprinted upward, reaching the second landing as the door burst open below. He didn't look back. There wasn't time to assess whether the man had a shot through the gap between the stairs. Practically bouncing off the wall, Raith reached the fourth landing—and his destination.

"Thirty seconds," Roark said, "before power flushes and security returns."

"Thanks for the update, not really what I need to hear right now," Raith retorted, blasting into the next hallway. Right away, he saw the glass doors leading into a private hangar filled with a half-dozen fancy yachts. He recognized the racing pinnace immediately from the downloaded files—a red and black dagger-like vessel suspended above the hangar floor by a few meters. A ladder led right to its cockpit.

"When the security drones fire up, I think you'll appreciate the heads up," Roark added.

Raith fired a script through Virtual; the doors slid open. He was glad the code worked as he passed through them—the glass was at least three to four inches thick. Not even his synthetic frame could have fractured that glass. Without waiting, he flew up the ladder, transmitted the ship's codes, and overrode its security protocols. Easy.

"Fifteen seconds."

"Stop it!" He dropped into the ship. Instead of plasti-glass, the ship used an experimental energy shield as the barrier between pilot and space. It even came with a Jump drive. Expensive indeed. He fired up the thrusters and repulsors, guided the ship toward the exit berth, and darted into the night sky.

"Three . . . two . . . one . . ."

Raith abruptly killed the ship's power, letting it nosedive toward the surface of Emerald Jewel.

"Are you insane?" Roark followed up the comment with a string of unintelligible curses.

"Don't talk to me right now, I'm focusing."

The ship dropped like a rock in water, plummeting. As Raith's perspective shifted, he watched the city's chaos coalesce beneath the tower. Public transports and private craft darted in predestined routes between high-rises, and his commandeered escape pod was heading straight for one traffic current. He quickly glanced upward toward the tower's hangar. It might have been his imagination, but he thought he saw the old man waving a fist. The security drones would immediately detect his power fluctuation as abnormal if outside a traffic lane. They might already see him, but his death drop was the only chance they wouldn't notice him. Just a big bird, right?

The mob of unsuspecting drivers approached. Hundreds of meters passed in mere seconds. Raith focused. Made the necessary estimations—approximation was all he had time for. When he was less than a few ship lengths from the virtual highway, he gunned the engines. A few horns blared, but the repulsors and inertial compensators did their magic, leveling the ship into the flow of other pilots.

"All right, time to swipe this ship." Raith pulled up a list of his favorite programs and dragged a counterfeit ID mask through Augmented Reality into the ship's operating system. Because he already used the ship's proper clearance codes, the computer didn't really resist receiving a new name. Seconds later, the craft was flying under Raith's banner as the *Snuggler*. No one ever suspects a ship called the *Snuggler* of being part of a burglary.

"All right." He plotted a trajectory out of the air highways and toward orbit. "I think I'm clear. What's our rendezvous?"

"The moment you rearranged our plan, I pulled out to safe distance. If you're good to fly yourself home, then we meet at the *Iron Dagger* on our own time."

"I'm completely ok with that plan."

"Then see you in a bit, comrade."

Raith tapped his fingers on the ship's console. It was a beauty, all right. It had been quite a few months since he piloted anything. Maybe he'd take a few extra minutes to do some passes through the canyons of Emerald Jewel's moons before meeting back up with the crew.

* * *

"You stole his race ship?"

"It was my best avenue of escape."

"But his race ship? Are you insane?"

"Hey, it's not my fault you don't tell us the identity of our targets prior to our stakeouts. How was I supposed to know we were robbing Indio Rodrigo, infamous pirate and Solar Sprint champion?"

Raith leaned back into the couch. They were in the *Iron Dagger's* lounge, the rest of the crew standing idly—awkwardly—against the wall. Roark sat in a chair a few paces away, and across the table from Raith, Captain Carisa Khan glared. "I don't think you understand how much you botched up this job, Raith. This isn't something to laugh off. Do you see any of us laughing?"

Raith pointed at Benjo, who was sticking his finger in an ear. "Well, he always has a weird smirk on his—"

Carisa slammed her fist on the table. "I swear to Jack, I would throw you out a damn air lock if I didn't feel bad for the space whales that would kill themselves for listening to your tirades."

Raith's head swiveled back and forth, unsure what to say. The rest of the crew stared at the ground. Carisa had always been a pain in his neck. Yeah, he owed her for quite a bit. Lots of debts paid off because of her. But her words once again re-affirmed his need to escape three weeks ago.

"Well, how about we call it even," Raith said.

"What?" her eyes turned into even sharper knives.

"You keep the racing pinnace after we finish this mission, and all is forgiven."

"You were under the assumption it was yours?" she asked.

"Well, right now, I have the codes, and I own the counterfeit identity over the ship. So yes, it's mine."

She tilted her head. "I hate you, you know that, right?"

"Yeah, but you also love me. And need me. For the rest of this mission."

"Well, since Rodrigo's been tipped off, yes, yes I do. For something incredibly specific. Everyone else? Out."

The other crewmembers looked at her, confused. They were certainly enjoying her reprimand of the one SI on the *Iron Dagger*, and somehow, Raith had ruined their fun. Well, they didn't deserve fun. Maybe Roark, but he was a bit too pompous for an organic, too.

"I said *out*." Khan waved her hands wildly in the air. They all rushed from the room.

"All right," Raith said, "So what's this about? What's the plan?"

Carisa sighed. "Why do you make everything so difficult?"

"I am who I am."

"Obviously. All right. Look. The plan *was* to use the information you acquired to hijack Rodrigo's Exo shipments tomorrow. Well, he's been tipped off now, and we need a distraction. You're going to be that distraction." The woman stood, waving her ochre hands in the air. A moment later, a map of the Emerald Jewel system appeared between them, their AR displays linking and showing the same simultaneous data.

Raith immediately identified the shipment routes entering and exiting the system near its furthest gas giant, Tauras. Curiously enough, the map *also* noted details regarding an upcoming race starting in orbit around Lune, a moon of Tauras. Raith wasn't sure he liked the implications.

"Rodrigo is going to expect us to outright assault one of his haulers.

They're big ships, you know, piloted by those immobile SIs you despise so much." She zoomed in not on the cargo routes, but on Lune. "So here's where you come in. That racing ship you hijacked?"

"Commandeered for a better cause, that's the phrasing I prefer," Raith interjected.

Carisa raised an eyebrow. "Yes, well, fortunately, there's an interesting event occurring in Lune's orbit tomorrow. Open season, open enrollment. Any ship can join, provided its throttle can be regulated according to the race's specifications."

"All right, and . . ."

She smiled.

Raith did not like her smile.

"And, we'll be entering you, and your new ship, the *Snuggler*. Really, the *Snuggler*? We'll be entering it. You'll use the race to create a distraction at the right time, and we'll use the distraction to snag one of the haulers. Sound simple enough?"

"Quite."

She clicked her tongue. "Good. You might want to prep. Your career as a professional space racer starts tomorrow."

* * *

All it took was an entry form submitted before midnight. Ten hours later, Raith was sitting inside the *Snuggler* in orbit above Lune and Tauras. Twenty-five other participants waited in ships nearby, less than a kilometer separating the entire pack.

"All right racers, you've all read the rules, but here's the deal." The announcer had been droning for over an hour, and his nasally nonsense continued. "The leader sets the course. There are buoys scattered throughout the Tauras sub-system, and whenever you're in the lead, you select the next buoy destination, and the race is on. First pilot to the next buoy selects the next buoy. First pilot to win three buoys wins the race. Simple enough, yes?"

The man had said the words at least ten times by now. Raith clicked in an affirmative through the *Snuggler*'s console and leaned back, waiting for the race to start.

He'd flown ships essentially ever since the day his mobile synthetic framework rolled off the production line, but Raith had never once raced. The thought of participating in a race never really garnered much attraction in his mind. He knew at least a few SIs raced, but the thrill—the adrenaline rush experienced by humans—wasn't exactly a feeling non-biologicals could match.

Still, as he sat waiting for the green light, Raith relished the tension building within his neural network. He couldn't deny it. He was excited. He was the only SI in the race; the judges must have found his application quite peculiar. It made him feel special. He stood out. There were quite a few famous SIs throughout humanity, but no one had ever heard of Raith before. His digital synapses fired, considering the possibilities. He dared to dream, just for a moment, of what it would be like to strike out on his own as a professional racer.

Then, the lights began ticking down. First red, then yellow, then . . .

Green.

Raith cycled through his preordained commands, and the ship immediately followed the plotted path. The first buoy was a few hundred thousand kilometers away, situated between the halves of a tiny moon cracked eons ago in half by an unknown ancient force of nature. Every other ship bee-lined directly for the lunar hemispheres, but Raith took a slightly different arc, his vector guiding him first dozens—then hundreds—then thousands of kilometers closer to the gas giant. The other pilots followed the arc of orbit; Raith used the gaseous gravitational pull to assist in acceleration.

It worked.

Almost.

Immediately, the *Snuggler*'s velocity skyrocketed, its unorthodox route creating the start of a wide parabola toward the moon. "All right, let's see what this ship can really do," Raith muttered. At the zenith of the arc, he pushed the throttle more aggressively, flaring the booster engines to their max. The ship practically squealed with delight as it zipped toward the two moons. While the race coordinators had capped max velocity, they hadn't capped max acceleration, and Rodrigo's ship could *soar*.

No—not Rodrigo's ship. Raith's ship. He bought the *Snuggler* fair and square three weeks ago. That's what his paperwork said.

Distance ticked by on his HUD as he neared the first buoy. His route was longer, but it had given him the head start he needed. He slipped through the buoy ten kilometers ahead of the next pilot.

"All right, Captain Khan," Raith said over their private connection. "We're good to go." A suite of buoy targets appeared on his screen. He transmitted their locations to the *Iron Dagger*. "I have ten seconds to select the target. For now, they'll all shadow me."

Simple static, then Carisa said, "Far side of Tauras. Far side of the largest moon, actually. Hera."

"Got it." He locked in the buoy. "Send me the transport routes. I just need to pull as many ships with me as possible."

"Overlaying the current trajectories," said Roark's voice, rather than the captain's.

A few seconds later, a series of vectors appeared, transposing over the representation of the Tauras sub-system already displayed inside the *Snuggler*'s cockpit. Three haulers, all drifting lackadaisically away from a massive mining platform at the edge of the gas giant's atmosphere. They'd picked up their Exo shipments, presumably, and were now moving slowly out of the planet's gravity well before making their Jumps to distant ICH systems.

And all three sat between the racing pack and their next buoy.

Raith completed his slow burn arc, Tauras now centering itself in his field of vision. Two of its larger moons eclipsed his view; otherwise, the path toward the haulers was clear, with the next buoy on the far side of the planet.

"All right friends," he muttered, "let's go." The *Snuggler* accelerated, and in tandem, the other twenty-five pilots followed his arc. "Idiots." He read their profiles before the race. They were all amateurs, like he was. Because he won the first buoy, they would assuredly believe *he* knew the best vectors to follow. "Idiots," he repeated.

As the ship's computer quietly calculated and recalculated the complex trajectories and possible paths, Raith leaned back and enjoyed the ride. The ship's velocity continued to accelerate, nearing the capped speed of three hundred thousand kilometers per hour. With the next buoy a good million kilometers away, he had some time to relax. Though, not too much time—the haulers essentially bisected the vector.

He slightly drifted the ship off the "ideal" route the computer proposed, certain the pilots behind him would assume he had a smarter navigational system when it came to factoring the gravitational pulls of the planet and its satellites. The new route brought him within three kilometers of the path of the haulers.

"All set," Raith said to the *Iron Dagger*. Distraction in about . . . fifty minutes."

"You've almost made up for your mistake yesterday," Carisa said.

"I'm glad I can make you proud." Raith sneered. It was one of his favorite facial expressions to mimic as an SI.

The minutes ticked by. Three pilots actually deviated from his "alternative" route, but they were slower, and the rest followed him like lemmings. The haulers ignored the race, presumably assuming the officials placed a restriction on intersecting commercial routes. They also assumed Raith would follow the rules.

They were within ten thousand kilometers of the haulers. Two minutes more, and he'd be leading two dozen racers right across the path of the transports. "Well, we can always make this a little bit more interesting." Raith changed the trajectory once again. "Time to scare an exo-pusher."

To his surprise, the pack continued their similarly suicidal path, following him. True idiocy. Or, they were simply adrenaline junkies. Always impossible to tell the difference.

Five-hundred kilometers.

Three-hundred kilometers.

One-hundred kilometers.

Fifty.

Twenty.

Five.

One.

Raith tilted the *Snuggler*, its canopy facing the bow windows of the hauler. He was going too fast to wave, but he hoped someone freaked out as he came within a few hundred meters of the ship.

The problem: the hauler's trajectory didn't change. It continued moving. As Raith passed in front of it, milliseconds later, it filled the space Raith had blazed through. And it was a larger ship—at least three to four kilometers in length. It was moving quite slow. A fraction of the race pace. Passing between Raith and the other racers, it created a roadblock.

His opponents truly were idiots.

Well, at least a few were.

Three racers slammed into the hull of the exo-hauler, their signals beeping out of existence. The rest of the pack deviated their vectors sufficiently to skirt the top of the massive cargo ship. But the damage was done. The vessel cut its thrusters.

"I could kiss you," Carisa shouted over the comm. "Raith, you're a genius."

"Why thank you, but please don't. Now I think I'll finish this race, even though they've probably just disqualified me."

As he finished the comment, an alarm sounded. "Excuse me, what?"

The two other massive vessels were deviating from their route, heading in Raith's direction.

"They'll never catch me." A communication request appeared on his HUD—coming from the second hauler. "What the hell, this might be entertaining." He accepted the request.

"That's my ship, you tinny-tumbled bastard of a synthetic!"

"Oh, hello Rodrigo."

"You and Carisa have messed with the wrong man," he said. "Thanks for springing my trap."

"I don't know what you're talking about, *man*," Raith replied. "I'm just a racer in a ship I bought three weeks ago. You don't know me."

"Doesn't matter. You messed with the wrong retired pirate."

The comment triggered a thought in Raith's mind. He recalled the books on the man's shelf and the initial plan designed by Carisa—he considered it all. Rodrigo knew her name immediately. Of course. The plan targeted him *because* he was a former pirate. Was it revenge? Did she target him because he wouldn't call law enforcement or the ICH for backup? Was he wanted as well?

How did Carisa know Rodrigo?

Raith watched his race trajectory. If he wanted, he could far outclass the hauler's velocity, though—

Another alarm sounded. On his display, red lights shouted: RACE CANCELED.

Great.

"You should check race sponsors more closely, you insignificant speck." Rodrigo disconnected from the call. A moment later, a dozen blips appeared, flying away from the second hauler at obscene velocities.

"You fired *missiles* at me?" Raith knew the old pirate couldn't hear him, but the words were still worth shouting into the void. "No. No no no. This is now how I'm going out. *Iron Dagger*, where are you? Did you know this would happen?"

Silence.

"*Iron Dagger?*"

"We may not have . . . checked the armaments of his haulers," Carisa said.

"What the—"

Before he finished the comment, his comrades appeared a few thousand kilometers away. Their commandeered ICH frigate shone brilliantly on his scopes, and its trajectory immediately veered toward him.

"Don't you worry Raith," Roark said, "we've got point defense cannons already spraying at full capacity. Transmitting their ranges now, stay clear."

"Much appreciated."

"Get yourself home, it's not safe out there."

Raith stared one last time at the distant buoy on his scopes. The race was over. The other pilots were fleeing the scene. He'd enjoyed it, while it lasted. "On my way. I'll loop around to starboard."

The battle between the *Iron Dagger* and its quarry commenced, kinetics and missiles dancing across the Tauras sky. By now, ICH security forces in orbit around Emerald Jewel must have been notified, but it would take them a few hours to mobilize and reach the planet. By then, they'd be long gone.

Hopefully.

Regardless, Raith would need to try this whole racing thing again another time.

* * *

Raith arrived on the *Iron Dagger*'s bridge a few minutes later, after docking the *Snuggler* inside the frigate's hangar.

"Raith, I need you on shields," Carisa yelled over the usual clamor of the ops room. "Hop to it!"

"Aye, aye, captain," Raith said. Sliding into an ops couch, he joined Varin, a young, lightly-tanned woman from Mars. "What's our situation?"

"Deflectors are operating at peak efficiency, but they're scattering us with electromagnetic pulses in an attempt to scatter electrons and distort integrity," said Varin. "Be on guard to drop and reactivate at a moment's notice."

"Understood."

His AR network quickly parsed data from the ship's central computers. Captain Carisa declined working with a ship-bound SI—one of the reasons he appreciated working on the *Iron Dagger* over previous employers. He hated living inside another one of his kind. Instead, hyper-advanced algorithmic AI provided them with all the support they needed. And right now, the system was feeding him tactical readouts and awaiting his commands. It did most of the work, including the actual intensive calculations.

But it still required orders from living, thinking minds.

The battle before them was simple. The *Iron Dagger* faced down the large hauler—a transport ship apparently outfitted with a sufficiently advanced armament of weapons capable of holding their own against their firepower. Fortunately, the other two haulers were essentially dead in the water, unarmed and unshielded. They were civilian transports, after all. Rodrigo had converted the third into a covert privateer.

The *Iron Dagger* utilized mostly kinetic weapons, including point defense cannons and rail gun batteries. Its true specialty came from its shields—experimental technology developed within the past decade, the new particle shields could disintegrate even some missiles before they reached a ship's hull. Unlike in the Virtual games loved by too many humans, the shields didn't form a perpetual bubble around the vessel.

The shields needed to be aimed.

But this battle was straight-forward. Rodrigo had one ship. Didn't they simply need to keep the shields pointed toward his vessel and call it a day?

And then he saw the pattern.

In arrhythmia, the enemy ship erratically pulsed, with no clear rhyme or reason. With each pulse, a few seconds later, shield integrity wavered—but not entirely. The invisible electron blasts only fractured part of the shield wall. And it didn't affect the generators at all.

"All right," he said, "I see what you're talking about. And there's no pattern?"

"None that I can discern," said Varin. "It truly feels random. I think it *is* random."

"Hmm." Raith watched their shields fracture; a missile slipped through the crack, but a point defense cannon intercepted the projectile before it reached the *Iron Dagger*. "There's got to be a solution. A way for us to counter their tactic. Otherwise, they'll slip a blow through eventually."

"Or we just hold long enough till we hit them hard enough for it to count."

"True."

Raith continued watching, shifting the shields with no discernible goal other than to confuse. The *Iron Dagger* continued on its vector, intent on nearing the lead cargo hauler. He'd seen the boarding party in the hangar after docking the *Snuggler*. What a bold move, hijacking an entire hauler.

Whatever. He was content to reposition shields for an hour or two.

"Attention, *Iron Dagger*." The voice rang through the entire ship.

"Who's letting him do that?" Carisa said. "What the hell?"

"This is Commodore Rodrigo speaking. You should all know my name. My reputation."

"Should we?" Raith muttered.

"No idea," retorted Varin. "I've never heard of him."

"Well, you're nineteen, that's not that surprising."

"Shut it you old tinny."

"Shut it both of you." The captain's voice cracked through the bridge. "Unless you can tell me how he's doing that."

"I am willing to offer you all amnesty," Rodrigo said. "Let's cut to the chase. The meat of it all. The reason I'm here, and not back home, relaxing with a glass of bourbon. Do you know how much it costs to import real bourbon? You've all ruined my night. Anyway, If you simply turn over your synthetic friend and return my ship."

The bridge of the *Iron Dagger* silenced. Through the data streams on his AR display, Raith glanced around the room, noting the furtive stares. Varin, for her part, tried her best *not* to look at him. Roark, from the helm, couldn't do anything *other* than look at him.

And the Captain, she sat in her chair, pondering the question.

And there it was. Raith saw it in her eyes. She was actually considering it. She might turn him over.

Seconds passed. The firefight continued, lighting up the Tauras sky with plumes of rapidly dispersing fire and smoke.

"Do you take me for a traitor to my own crew?" Carisa said. "You should know me better than that."

But she'd taken a long time to arrive at her answer, Raith noted. He logged the thought away before returning to the task at hand.

"So be it," They heard no more from Rodrigo.

"Captain, what's the plan?" Raith said.

"Just focus on the shields. Do your job, I'll do mine."

Raith considered a retort but decided not to bark back at her right after she contemplated selling him to their opponent. Returning to the shields, he queued in a few commands and sat back to watch the fireworks for a moment.

Was there a rhythm? Or was the enemy firing the electron pulse erratically precisely to confuse their shields? He watched. Counted. Found no pattern.

Yet . . .

"Varin, can you give me complete control for 120 seconds, starting in about thirty seconds, after I chart out a plan with the AI?"

"Sounds good," she said.

Even as she said the words, Raith submitted a concept script to the ship's computer. It pinged an affirmative, and a few seconds later, the full defensive plan was ready.

Varin glanced at him after she saw the blueprint for the next two minutes. "You're insane."

"You're just figuring that out now?" he said.

After their previous directions completed, Raith's new plan activated. For the first thirty seconds, the shields darted around the ship in a consistent path, covering railgun placements with a regular one-two-one-two pattern. Raith watched . . . and saw the shift. After fifteen seconds, the enemy's pulse weapon transformed its pattern. "Perfect," he muttered. "All right, now for phase two."

The *Iron Dagger*'s shields oscillated like a strobe light on an electrodance floor. Instead of with rhythm, the flicker was truly random, as designed by Raith's script.

The electron pulse gun fired more erratically, its angle shifting. Sometimes it connected with a shield, other times its quantum-sized projectiles hit nothing but space. And then—a tiny explosion ignited on the side of Rodrigo's ship.

"It overloaded," Raith said. "Shields full strength and full capacity!"

"You're a freaking genius!" Varin whooped in glee, and the bridge received notice—the boarding party was ready for its drop. They were in range, ready to utilize the shields as partial cover for the drop ship, and—

The two haulers actually containing Exo exploded. Rodrigo's ship vanished, Jumping into the beyond.

"Well shit," Raith whispered.

* * *

The crew rested in the lounge, all watching the replay of the battle. Carisa paced, walking back and forth through the AR projection of the Tauras system. The *Iron Dagger* had Jumped immediately following the battle, ending its transit approximately one light-year outside Emerald Jewel's solar system in the middle of dark space. No one could find them unless they knew exactly where to look.

"What went wrong today?" Carisa asked. "How did we fail?"

The room remained silent.

"No one has an answer? Maybe Raith, perhaps?"

"Excuse me?" he said. "I did everything right. I won the race, I fixed our shield problem, I—"

"No, no, no," she said. "All of this was your fault. We could have jumped them unawares, we could have had those haulers without them knowing we were coming, but no, you botched it all the way back on Emerald Jewel."

Raith stood, staggering toward the woman. "You look here," he said. "I joined this crew because you needed someone of my particular talents, don't you start blaming me for something that wasn't my fault." He stuttered for a moment, considering whether he should declare his next thought. It might be unfounded, but he was pretty sure he had a basis for its conclusion. "This was never about the Exo, was it? It was about revenge. You knew Rodrigo. He made it pretty clear we should know him, at least, but none of us did. So how did you know him? Former lover? Hey, not going to judge, though he is old. Father? Uncle? Did you sail under him? All I know, he knew I was coming. He was ready when I showed up in his apartment. Like he'd been expecting this for a while." Raith stepped back and leaned against the table.

"I should have sold you to him." She seethed, her body rising in fury.

"SIs have existed for almost two centuries, and y'all are still talking about us like we're property," Raith said. "To be bought and sold, when we've never been bought and sold. You make me sick. I thought you were better than that." He stormed out of the lounge. To her credit, Carisa actually called out an apology as he fled. She might be a pirate, but she wasn't a terrible person. Not all the time.

Raith wandered the halls of the *Iron Dagger*, letting his feet guide him to wherever they may lead. Before long, he arrived at the frigate's tiny hangar, where the *Snuggler* nestled into a berth beside two drop ships. He examined the small craft for a moment, recalling the thrill experienced during the race. It called to him.

The *Iron Dagger* had been his home for two years. He'd flown with other crews in the past. He was nearing a century in age, and it was about time he found something new to do with his life. He'd always been a pilot, whether running with "respectable" companies or otherwise. Yet now, he saw a new opportunity.

A new career, to forge a name for himself. All of the ICH, both human and SI alike, would know the name Raith.

He climbed the ladder into the *Snuggler*. "Well, good thing this little vessel has a Jump drive. Thank you Rodrigo."

Raith had no belongings. He was an SI—everything he needed was contained on his personal servers. He transmitted his resignation papers as the ship dropped away from the frigate. By the time they realized he was gone, they'd be unable to track him.

They might come for him eventually. He still owed a few debts to more than half the crew, including Carisa. But it was time for something new. He'd find his own team. And he'd find a few races to win.

To actually win.

No more living the same life, raid to raid, job to job. It was time to live for himself.

The Treeherder

Each day, the same.

Always the same.

The world, their garden, perfect in every way.

The treeherder rose from his bed among the flowers and walked beneath the giant trunks of their forebearers. Thousands upon thousands rooted beneath the mountain. These ancient ones found a home in the treeherder's garden, and they were grateful and more than willing to give them a final refuge.

The treeherder's long limbs, spindly and craggly, landed gently between bush and fern. From tree to tree they walked, checking their branches, their seeds, their leaves. For a thousand rotations, the treeherder had welcomed new souls. Another was arriving today.

After finishing their rounds, the treeherder arrived at the edge of the forest. They stared toward the sun, its blazing light giving warmth and comfort. Striking across the daytime sky, a white comet blazed in glory. Who would it be today?

As it neared, the white streak revealed itself not as a comet, but a seed, thrown from afar by a worldship dancing between the stars. The treeherder waited, raising their branches in a welcome embrace. In a massive loop, the seed flung itself upward, slowed, and dropped to the ground, landing comfortably in the field the treeherder selected for it.

They furtively walked forward as the smoke and steam cleared. The seed's carapace fell to the ground, revealing an ancient one resting inside. Its old bones, grey and cracked, waited for the lush soil of the treeherder's garden.

"Welcome home," the treeherder said. "I am here for you, ready for you to begin again."

* * *

Each day, the same.

Always the same.

The world, their garden, providing rebirth and restoration.

The treeherder approached the most ancient of all ancient ones. Its trunk spanned fifty seeds, and its branches created a canopy worthy of the greatest gardens across the galaxy. And from its branches hung dozens of saplings. And all of them were ready.

The treeherder placed their swindled arm on the trunk of the ancient one. Through a conversation beyond sound and concept, they discussed what was to come. What the saplings needed. Where they must go. And as they conversed, the saplings began to droop, to drip, to fall to the loamy soil below.

The treeherder released their connection with the ancient one. The saplings wobbled on uncertain limbs. Their eyes, young with excitement, contained the wisdom of the most ancient of ancient ones. The knowledge. The philosophies. Everything they needed to continue the legacy of their progenitor.

"My children," said the treeherder, "welcome to my garden. Together, we will prepare you for the stars."

* * *

Each day, the same.

Always the same.

The world, their garden, beautiful in every way.

The saplings darted about the forest, inquisitive and creative in their pursuits. They shaped flowers and plants into curious forms, some functional, some . . . not so much. But the treeherder didn't correct them. They were learning. They were reforming. They were becoming their own.

Saplings followed the treeherder every day on their rounds, watching them water and groom the ancient ones. When another seed arrived, they stared in awe as its carapace dissolved into fertilizing dust.

It was good to have saplings in the garden again. They brought new life.

* * *

Each day, the same.

Always the same.

The world, their garden, living for all time.

* * *

The treeherder awoke. Something was wrong. They sensed it—inferno. Apocalypse. Death. All of it was coming.

Their worst nightmare.

Rushing from their bed, they entered the forest, checking on the ancient ones trunk-by-trunk. They sensed it too. The impending doom. From where it came, they did not know.

The treeherder reached the end of the forest, in the field where the newest seeds took root. Nothing appeared out of the ordinary. Unless . . .

They glanced toward the starry sky.

A soundless light show illuminated the moon. A battle—but between whom? The worldships knew to keep their conflicts away from the gardens. They would not dare set themselves in orbit around consecrated spaces. Some of the most recent seeds whispered of new beings walking the sky, jumping from star to star. Until now, the treeherder had believed the rumors to be mere speculation. For thousands of years, their roots had spread throughout the stars alone.

But the fire in the sky said otherwise.

A lance of red light stabbed through one a massive dark object, and even from thousands of branches away, the treeherder recognized the fatal wound. The hull of the alien ship fractured, cracked, and lost its hold on a stable orbit.

The treeherder's leaves bristled. They watched in horror as the hull of the behemoth vessel fell toward their garden. But they couldn't wait. They must collect the saplings. They must encourage the ancient ones to drop any other saplings before it was too late. The ancient ones couldn't be saved; but they could save their children.

* * *

Each day, the same.

Always the same.

The world, their garden, blazing. Engulfed. Ruined.

The saplings huddled inside the cave, peeking out of its shadowed holes. The treeherder stood at the entrance, watching the smoke devastate the mountainside. The massive vessel had pummeled into the land branches upon branches away, but it ignited the world in smoke and ash. Fire spread. They had no time to save the garden.

The ancient ones were perishing. They could hear their cries for help, not only from their bark and roots, but from their saplings, watching their progenitors die in agony.

The treeherder crept to the back of the cave. Purple fungus ignited the way, recognizing their master. Reaching a large cavern, the saplings in tow, they found the bulbous seed they sought.

Resting their hand on its bark, they conversed with the waiting lifeform. It was the lifechild of a worldship, ready and waiting for the treeherder in case of the unthinkable.

In case of an apocalypse.

The world burned. But truth had revealed itself to the treeherder. These new beings who walked the stars, they believed themselves above all life, willing to crush and burn the holiest of holy places. The treeherder would reunite these saplings with the worldships. Then, they would embark on a crusade to destroy these criminals.

The lifechild writhed, receiving its commands. Satisfied, the treeherder directed the saplings to stay inside the cave. They returned to the entrance, leaving the children behind. With purpose, they strode down the mountainside, walking through the ashy remains of their garden. Storm clouds billowed, and as they reached their former home, rain pattered the smoky remains of the thousands of ancient ones they once protected.

Beyond the garden, beyond the field for new seeds, the treeherder continued to walk. Their destination was distant, but they needed to see the truth.

They needed to see the faces of those who would wantonly commit genocide.

They arrived, after many hours, at the crash site. They didn't know what to expect. From afar, they watched, as a dozen fleshy beings darted about the wreckage.

There were survivors.

Standing beside a boulder, motionless, the treeherder took it all in. The beings were hairless, except for a patch atop their heads. They wore strange cottony coverings with mismatched colors. The creatures were a motley crew, and they looked . . . weak.

These few would die on this planet. Its carnivorous wildlife would guarantee it. The treeherder turned away. They knew the image of their quarry. Now it was time to find all of them, out there among the stars, and make them pay for their present, past, and future atrocities.

They were the treeherder. They had lived a million years, passing from seed to ancient one to sapling to seed. Their soul knew the history of the galaxy. They would protect its future, too, from those who couldn't be bothered to protect the most beautiful minds to ever exist.

Each day, the same.

Always the same.

The world, their garden, it had been perfect in every way. But now . . . to war.

Remnants

The breeze tussled his hair as he sat under the oak tree, staring out across the field of dandelions. Through the leaves, the sun shone brightly, though not too hot and not too cold.

This day could last forever, Jacob thought.

He continued reading the book sitting in his lap—*On Liberty*, By John Stuart Mill. A philosopher over four centuries past. Jacob read, page after page, enjoying the bliss of the perfect weather surrounding him in quiet peace.

I feel as if there is something I need to do. How did I get here?

Central Park, New York City, on a park bench overlooking the lake. Families sat on red and white picnic blankets on the hillside, their children giggling and laughing at the ducks splashing in the water. The smell of pretzels and hot dogs drifted through the air, a pleasant aroma to Jacob's senses. He looked across the park, at the towering skyline surrounding him, searching for the GarVoque Tower. His home.

I need to go home. For some reason, however, the concept was counterintuitive. His mind was playing tricks with him. *You don't need to go home Jacob, right here is where you are meant to be . . . but I am tired, I wish to sleep . . . no you don't. You can sleep right here.* His will won, but it took all his effort to stand.

He walked at a leisurely pace along the path, a nagging voice in his head trying to call him back to the bench. As he looked away from the families, their sounds subsided. But when Jacob looked back toward the lake, the sounds resumed. *That's not how sound works . . .*

As he walked along the path, he hummed the tune to his favorite song, the beat going in rhythm with the trickling of the water in the fountain to his left.

"Jacob." A feminine voice, calling from toward the lake, much more loudly than other sound. He turned to face the one who called his name. No one was there.

How did I get here?

The snow was blinding, but still, he pressed on through the storm. He'd reach his apartment building eventually, but more than likely, he'd be late for Christmas again this year. Peter was going to kill him, even if the man was going to love his gift—a necklace with three diamonds, the middle one slightly bigger than the other two.

The fresh leather in the new car smelled wonderful, all of the electronics running at full speed and efficiency.

Why am I driving a new car in a snowstorm? Something pushed the thought to the back of his mind. He didn't need to worry about that fact. Just keep driving. He'll be home soon.

His vehicle handled the winds well enough—but nothing escaped a blinding whiteout. He drove the curves along the mountain road (since when were there mountains in Manhattan?) at a slow and steady pace. He approached a stop sign, looking both ways, and rolled through it, unsure if his wheels could handle a full stop on the icy road. He glanced to the right.

A loud horn boomed.

White light overwhelmed the cabin of Jacob's car.

He slammed on the brakes.

Thankfully, the car stopped, even on the ice. The truck slid by, mere inches in front of his bumper.

"What the hell, man!" Jacob tried to yell the words, but no sound left his lips. He stared down the road; it was quite straight and narrow. There was no way he could have missed the truck when he looked.

I need to find out what is happening to me. Where was I again before this road trip?

"Jacob."

A voice called for him from the backseat. He whipped his head back, staring at the dark unlit seat, but no one was there. No one at all.

Where am I going?

Jacob leaned against a metal fence. Sand scratched his leg. No—burned his leg. The sun, scorching, roasted his skin second-by-second.

A massive ship towered high above him, even though its base was at the bottom of the hill. Its construction was almost completed; only a few modules remained to attach to the vessel. Massive machines were painting red letters on its hull, but he could not read their words.

He squinted.

Contractors ran about at a steady pace, engineers barking orders at those around them. Jacob turned away from the ship, its immensity for some reason not surprising him whatsoever. A question nagged, though. Why build it down here, rather than in orbit? That didn't seem right. For a brief moment, the world flickered—the vacuum of space replacing the desert landscape. He gasped for breath—his eyes bulged.

The desert returned.

To his left, a security checkpoint allowed works in and out of the gigantic facility. He noticed a family in the midst of a dispute. The small child sobbed, his father kneeling hugged him goodbye.

"Do you have to go?" the boy sniffled, clinging to the small stuffed bear in his hands. He dropped it into the sand as his father went to stand up, grasping his father's pant leg instead. "No! I won't let you go. You won't ever come back!"

The father still said nothing. The boy's other father pulled their son away. The man turned to leave, but he glanced toward Jacob.

They wore the same face.

Jacob tried to rush forward, to grab the son, to sweep him into his arms, but the sand glued him in place. He could not move. He was trapped.

The son wailed as his father swept him into his arms. *What is his name?*

Why can't I remember his name?

Both parents said nothing to each other. Child and father walked into the desert, leaving footprints in the loose sand.

Jacob's attention shifted away, more from pain than desire. A woman in a purple dress was leaning against the fence on the other side of the security checkpoint. She made eye contact with him, her oddly shining eyes boring straight through him.

He looked away, hoping she did not notice his gaze.

He looked up again.

She was gone.

Bewildered, he looked around, trying to see how she could have disappeared, but there was no cover. It was still an empty, sandy desert. The fence prevented people from coming in without authorization, and the desert stretched for many miles.

"Jacob. We need to talk."

Where had he heard that voice before?

He turned around.

The woman waited, ten feet away, staring.

He walked toward her, hoping she would speak again, but she kept staring, staring, staring.

"Miss, were you speaking to me just then?" He asked politely, or at least he thought he asked. Once again, no words emitted from his mouth. Jacob looked around, suddenly leery of what he was doing. Someone was watching everything. Controlling everything. He was trapped in a prison of his own creation, but also *their* creation. He needed to escape.

Now.

Wait, how do I know that?

The woman did not respond, unfortunately. She held the same blank stare for a lifetime.

You will escape. I will help you.

Men and women rushed about in a frenzy. The captain of the ship (how did he know he was on a ship?) shouted various orders, yet Jacob paid them no heed. He was focused on something else. A job. His job. He was sitting at a console, thinking perhaps he would find the answer he sought within the ship's computer system. No, that's not right. He was the pilot. He was supposed to be flying the ship, not searching for information on its servers. Sadly, the display before him streaming nonsensical data in a language he could not comprehend, flying across the screen in all directions at a million million bits a second. He tried to focus, but his mind clouded.

Someone is trying to contact you! Focus, Focus, Focus.

A cup of water appeared in his hand. He stared down at it, the out-of-place glass drinking vessel cold to the touch. (On a ship, all cups should be metal or plastic. Right?) He shook his head in confusion.

A drink wouldn't hurt, he thought, and he took a sip. The cold liquid rushed through his mouth, past his tongue and down his throat, invigorating every cell. Jacob looked around the bridge.

Scales fell from his eyes, revealing the hidden reality of the surrounding world. *I am the only one in the room.*

Sure, visages and reflections of people—people he knew—moved about the bridge. Except they were not people. Behind the façade, a grotesque copy, a snarled soul, stared back. The captain's lips were fake, completing a cartoonish expression on the man's face. The navigator—her hair seemed artificial, even with it dropping well past her shoulders. The co-pilot's eyes, staring directly at Jacob, were an unearthly green, as if they projected light instead of rebounding electrons.

Jacob closed his eye and breathed.

No air entered his lungs, but that was all right. In this world, he didn't need air.

After blinking, he stared blankly, ignoring all the blaring klaxons. A message materialized in the center of the screen.

Go to the airlock and walk outside. I will protect you.

Jacob could not believe what he was reading. *That would kill me!*

It will not. Trust me.

He looked around, taken aback upon realizing the captain hovered above him. "Lieutenant Fischer, what do you think you are doing?" the man shouted in Jacob's ear. "I ordered you to prep this vessel for preflight tests five minutes ago!"

Had it really been five minutes? Snapped out of his daze, Jacobs's hands went through the motions, as they had thousands of times before. He looked at the screen again, the phantom messages fading.

No.

What he was doing was wrong.

He looked up at the captain. The man's fake lips were quivering. Jacob reached for the man's arm, but his hand went right through, his body fading into ash. *This is weird. This is just really, really weird.*

Jacob rose. No one else on the bridge had seen what happened to the captain. The co-pilot was gone; he had never seen her leave her chair. He looked toward the corridor leading into the interior of the ship. A figure walked around the corner, out of sight, but he couldn't get a good glimpse of their features. An image of a girl in the desert flashed into his mind. *It's the same person, perhaps?* His mind finally comprehended what was happening.

None of this is real. It can't be real.

Now you're understanding.

The words flashed in front of his eyes as if an invisible TV hung in the air. Throwing his helmet to the floor next to the chair, he tried to run toward the corridor, but all he could manage was a slow jog, as if he was running through a pool of jelly. His boots eerily clanged against the metal of the floor, and he slowly made his way to the hallway leading toward the airlock. He passed into the upper levels of the cargo hold, running (if his motion could be considered running) along a narrow walkway high against the wall. He glanced down. An army of synthetics were placing citizens into their personal stasis pods. A wrangler pulled a horse into a larger space; a woman herded a group of sheep into another hold.

Jacob registered it all as he ran, unconsciously noting what was happening. He looked up once again. The figure—the woman—was running at full speed across a catwalk to reach the opposite end of the cargo hold. The metal walkway looked dangerously loose, but as he arrived at the metal bridge, he climbed onto it anyways. It swayed, but it held. He reached out to take hold of the railing, but it vanished straight through his hands. It was as if someone did not wish for him to accomplish whatever it was he was trying to do.

He looked to his right, noticing the many hanging cables ready to strangle his neck were he to fall. The floor stretched further away. The voices and animal squawks sounded as if they were coming from deep beneath an ocean.

Then he bridged the gap. *I don't even remember reaching the middle.* He quickly moved along the wall toward the airlock at the back end of the cargo hold. The woman was waiting. Before he reached her, she opened the door and walked inside, closing it behind her. The moment it shut, all hope fled his mind.

Winded. He was winded. He just needed to sleep. Fall to the ground, curl into a ball, and sleep. He yawned, his hand covering his mouth. Once again, no sound emitted from his vocal cords. He stumbled, looking up at the door only meters from him. The lights around him flickered and strobed, as if consciously trying to blind and distract.

He was at the door, its cold surface waking him up, even if only slightly. He reached for the lever to open it, triggering unfathomable pain.

Fire.

Fury.

A million needles, stabbing and tearing and scraping and smearing.

The flames spread up his arm. He pressed on, pushing the lever toward the floor as his heart exploded in agony. The door creaked. With each inch, the pain doubled. His mind screamed. *Please, let me wake up from this nightmare. Let it end!* He kept pushing.

The door opened.

He fell through the door . . .

Welcome to the land of the living, Jacob.

. . . and dropped straight onto the metal bulkhead of the cargo hold floor.

The pain was gone.

All gone.

He looked at his hand, expecting to burns, but the skin was flawless. Almost too flawless.

He glanced around. The hold was much emptier when he had seen it a few moments ago.

Wait, what exactly did I see a few moments ago?

Jacob remembered a voice. He remembered the captain billowing into ash, and his strange run through the ship. As he looked around, he honestly could not recall where he was or what in the world he was supposed to be doing. Realizing he was still lying on the hard floor, he sat up and hopped to his feet.

"Ow." Something pinched his neck. He pulled at it, and a blue liquid squirted across the floor. He assessed his limbs, finally noticing the IVs attached to his extremities, and he followed them back to their source. A stasis pod—he wasn't sure how he *knew* that's what it was—glowed, its hatch wide open. Green steam simmered from vents layering the back of the pod. Colored lights flashed along the panel on the left side of the door.

A striking image appeared in Jacob's mind, a flash of a door closing in front of him, sealing him inside the pod before embracing infinite darkness. As if he were watching another person, he recalled his body drifting into sleep.

What happened to me?

Sticky fluid spilled from the IVs as they tore away from his skin. He panted, leaned forward, and vomited a mixture of orange and yellow paste. Wheezing and coughing, his hands clenched his knees for a long moment of wretched realization of uncomfortable cluelessness.

Unclothed, he looked around for something to wear. As if the ship read his thoughts, a small panel in the floor popped open. The words on the drawer read "Jacob Fischer." *Me? My name?* He desperately wanted to hold onto what he sensed was his identity.

Inside the drawer was a flight suit, along with a small device. Instinctively, he donned the garment, and held the device in his hand, not sure of what it did. Another image flashed in his head, a simple picture of the small item fitting in an individual's ear. An earpiece.

Before he could place it in his ear, a light flashed across the upper portion of his vision. Looking up, he noticed the viewport along the wall of the cargo hold. His legs still shaky, he stumbled toward the window, peering out.

Millions of stars ignited the night sky above the backdrop of a beautiful planet down below. The cyans of ocean mixed with the emeralds of land. The sheer immensity of the scene left him in a stupor. *Where am I?*

Off to the right, another ship glowed, steadily making its way away from his location. Jacob instinctively pounded on the glass, calling out to the ship, but it was obviously of no use. The ship accelerated away, and with a blip, it disappeared, leaving him seemingly alone in the darkness. *What do I do now?*

He looked down at the earpiece still laying in his hand. It fit snuggly around his earlobe.

"It took you long enough," said a vaguely feminine voice. "I thought I would have to watch you forever staring uselessly at the tech needed to connect us. Good morning Jacob, I wish we could talk more, but we don't have a lot of time."

"Who . . . who are you?" he asked.

"Not important," she replied. "We have work to do, and only a few hours to do it. I lost a lot of time getting around the firewalls implanted within the recollection servers. First, do you remember who you are—and where you are traveling from?"

Jacob replied automatically. "First Lieutenant Jacob Fischer, pilot of the . . . the . . ." He tried to recall the ship's name. "I don't know. Nor from where I came."

"Damn it. Without the recollection phase, there really is little recovered." Her words were essentially nonsensical. "All right, Lieutenant, you're on a ship called the *Roanoke*. It's a colony ship. What information can you recall?"

More sporadic information bubbled to the surface. "The *Roanoke* is colony ship intended to land . . . somewhere."

"Destination isn't important. Good, these preliminary questions have given me enough information to imply that much of your practical knowledge is still intact. It appears much of your long term episodic memory seems to be lacking, however." More nonsense Jacob could not accurately comprehend. He nodded, going with the flow like a trained soldier. *Maybe that's what I was.*

As the voice continued to talk in a technical form he could barely understand, Jacob looked around the cargo hold completely for the first time. Along the wall running in both directions were hundreds of other stasis pods. Strangely, about one out of every four were empty.

"Jacob, are you listening?" the voice abruptly said.

"Look, I don't know who you are, but I understand enough to know that something is seriously wrong here. I can't pretend to know what is completely going on, but I know this much—my duty is to defend this ship at all costs. Tell me what I need to do to save the lives of those still aboard."

He almost thought he sensed a smile from the faceless entity. "That's the spirit I want to hear. About eighty-three hours ago, approximately one-hundred-thirty-seven individuals were removed from stasis prematurely. I was still asleep at the time, and they promptly began acquiring various supplies from throughout the ship. By my estimation, about sixty-four hours ago, a second vessel arrived in the system. It quickly dispatched a small cargo ship to attach itself to the airlock of the *Roanoke*. Over the next two days, the various supplies were quickly moved between the two ships, including important system functions vital to keeping the ship on its correct course as well as removing a vital system the sleeping pods depend on for awakening their occupants at the proper time."

She paused as if to catch her breath. "I awakened about twelve hours ago, as was the preprogrammed time set into the hardware of the *Roanoke*. I was able to observe the final cargo run and keep myself undetected. Once the last traitor left the ship, I began the process of awakening you."

Jacob took it all in, trying to get a grasp for the situation. So much flooded his head, but not enough information to comprehend the true stakes. But what was he to do? He couldn't just . . . walk away. He really only had one choice—solve the problem at hand. His memory slowly recalled important facts. The layout of the ship. Its functions. Its systems. And . . . and . . . he drew up blank on the final detail. "So who are you? You seem to know a lot about me, but I have no idea who you are."

"Just call me Jill. You'll understand much more soon enough. We've talked too long, however. We need to get to work."

Jacob flexed his hands. "Just tell me what I need to do."

* * *

Jacob climbed down the ladder, flashlight in his mouth. The generator above was humming to life, its reserve fuel cells reactivated. The access tunnel he was in was dark; the most necessary systems were using the majority of power. "That should do it," he said. "Is there anything else that needs to be done before we take this ship out of orbit?"

"My complete diagnostic checks show no other systems in need of necessary repair, though this maneuver is still going to be practically impossible to pull off without substantial damage to the ship. We'll run out of repulsor power in order to keep the life pods online about a thousand meters above the surface of the planet."

Jacob reached the bottom of the tunnel, kicking the access panel open to the hallway below. The ladder dropped to the floor, but he jumped down instead. "You're positive no other power can be diverted?"

"Well . . ." The synthetic mind paused for a few seconds.

"What is it?" he asked, slightly annoyed. He grabbed a few spare tools from the floor, stuffing them in the makeshift toolkit, before heading down the hallway toward the far end of the ship. Toward the bridge.

"The recovery mainframe," said Jill. "If we were to remove the power source from there and reroute it to the repulsors, we would have enough lift to bring the ship to within one-hundred meters from the surface before losing repulsor power. However, the decision would be irreversible. Memory recovery will be next to impossible without this system."

Jacob stopped in the middle of the corridor, placing his hand against the wall and considering the proposition. "How many people are likely to live if we don't reroute the power?" he asked.

"It's difficult to say," Jill said. "My preliminary models predict a fifty percent probability of the ship exploding upon impact, destroying everything inside, but the entire situation is also dependent on your piloting skills."

Jacob smirked. He could not remember much, but he knew he was a good—scratch that, better than good—pilot. Not just anyone could pilot these behemoth colony ships, even though they had mostly automated systems. Even with Jill doing most of the work, they needed the touch of a pro.

Without noticing his self-indulgent fantasy, Jill added, "Even with an exceptional landing maneuver, however, the impact still has a likelihood of killing close to one-hundred percent of the population about half the time, and the other scenarios do not look good either. A thousand meter impact even at an angle is just too much force for the hull to handle."

Jacob bit his lip and threw the wrench in his hand to the ground. It clanged with a loud metallic sound. "This is just wonderful." He left the wrench where it was and continued walking toward the bridge. "And with the rerouting of the power?"

"With an effective landing maneuver, the majority of my models predict a successful landing with only certain portions of the ship becoming majorly damaged. It appears the sleeping pods and cargo holds would stay mostly intact."

Jacob nodded, completely understanding the implications of his decision. Over the past day or so, as he worked on his repairs, the ship had been drifting, its orbit retrograde. Throughout his toil, barely any memories of Earth returned. Jill had provided some information, but there simply was not enough time, given the immediate nature of their work at hand. If he severed the power to the recovery mainframe, however, no one would recover their memories of Earth, except for what he assumed Jill knew. He would be making this decision not just for himself, but for all individuals on board . . . as well as their generations to follow. But if he didn't, most of them would die. And likely, the recovery mainframe would be destroyed during the crash, regardless.

"Remind me, why can't we wake them up now?"

"I told you." She sounded annoyed. He didn't know an AI, or SI, or whatever she was, could sound annoyed.

"You told me something, I'm not sure I understood."

"The recovery mainframe takes a lot of power. Cycling people in and out of stasis takes a lot of power. While they're in stasis, they using little to *no* power. And every electron counts."

"Got it, got it." Jacob frowned. "It seems to be a pretty obvious decision, then. Let's do it. You know, casually delete the memories of hundreds of people."

Jill emitted a noise in approval and acceptance. "Get to the bridge then. Let's take this ship down to the surface. I've marked on the navigation screen a suitable landing site—it'll bring us down on the dark side of the planet, with morning rising upon the finish of our descent, if all goes as planned."

Jacob was two steps ahead of her, running throughout the hallways, full of anticipation. *I have hundreds of lives in my hands. Possibly thousands, if I include their children to come.* "So Jill, are you ever going to reveal yourself to me beyond as a talking head in my ear?"

"You'll meet me on the bridge, I promise," Jill said. "I have a final favor to ask you."

"Cryptic," he muttered. On the way to the bridge, he passed his stasis pod. He had gotten used to the sleeping faces all around, but it still creeped him out considerably. At first, he hoped someone else could be awakened to help him, but Jill claimed that would take too much power given the firewalls in place to prevent early awakening. She said it had almost taken too much energy to revive Jacob. She reassured him, upon landing on the surface when they had expended all other power, the firewalls would break, and the individuals would awaken naturally.

The logic didn't really make sense, but he needed to trust the voice inside his head. She was the only truth he had to go on, especially given his lack of concrete memory beyond dreams from when he was in stasis. Who was he to question an omnipresent AI?

Jacob ran up the steps, the door sliding open as he reached it. The bridge was pristine, the pilot's chair sitting in the middle surrounded by the various other consoles. While the space had "viewports," it didn't have windows viewing the outside. Engineers purposely designed the bridge within the interior of the ship to keep those in control of the vessel relatively safe from harmful radiation and incidental impacts.

"Walk toward the computer mainframe located at the systems terminal," she said. Jacob obliged.

"I was stationed on this ship, just as you were, and was put to sleep, just as you were, once the ship's systems were completely functional and able to perform their duties until the time came to arrive in this system. When this ship lands, I will die, unless we create some sort of back-up of my mind."

Jacob scratched his head. "So let me guess. You need me to remove your memory systems once we land in order to ensure your survival until the time comes when we could somehow give you power again."

"Close." He sensed weariness in her voice. "I actually need you to remove me now. The amount of power I draw from the system is too much for the trip down to the surface. I have done the calculations, you'll need to do this maneuver without me."

Jacob nodded with comprehension. "Just tell me what I need to do."

"Get a small memory drive from the supply cabinet to the right. Plug it into the slot right below the access panel on this mainframe, and I'll perform the necessary download."

Jacob moved over to the cabinet, opening it and rummaging through the drawer. The instant he saw the device, the memory of what it was came to mind.. It was a dual-purpose storage drive and long-range communicator, solar-powered and capable of recharging itself nearly indefinitely.

Whatever happened down below on the planet, they would have time to save her mind.

The device in hand, he walked back to the computer mainframe and inserted it into the proper slot. "How long will this take?" he inquired.

Jacob received no answer, only a few beeps. Then, a few seconds later, he heard her voice again. "Everything is finished. Once you remove the drive, the point of no return begins. I will shut down all unnecessary systems for your flight to the surface."

"I understand," he said.

"Wait," she said. He paused to listen. "Jacob . . . good luck."

"Luck will have nothing to do with this flight," he said. "Besides, can an AI believe in luck?"

"I can believe in saying supportive phrases."

"I can practically hear your wink from here." He removed the drive.

* * *

The lights on the bridge dimmed. *Time for the inevitable.* Jacob nestled into the pilot's chair, his hands already re-familiarizing with the controls. In a distant past, he certainly knew everything possible about these systems, but those memories were locked away. Today, he relied on muscle memory. He needed to trust himself—not a particularly relaxing thought.

"Jill, I need you to—never mind." He was now in this alone, Jill's entire existence saved on a small memory drive in his pocket. Over the past day or so, he had grown quite attached to hearing her voice in his ear. Now she was gone, for what could be his entire lifetime, if he could not find a method to give power to any sort of computer capable of handling her program.

We'll just need to keep her safe, he thought.

A red light flashed. "Right, focus, I've got a small margin of error on this landing. *Roanoke,* let's see what you can do."

Jacob's fingers deftly moved across the control pad to his right, countless data fields scrolling on the screen. He pulled up digital representations of the planet, with a small beacon of light representing the position of the ship relative to the planet. View screens down below and in front of the pilot's chair showed the situation as it appeared directly outside the ship. Computers quickly calculated all the necessary numbers, such as the acceleration toward the planet, its gravitational pull, and rotation. He needed to account for everything as he brought the ship in for its crash landing upon the surface.

Usually, he'd have a crew to keep track of all the other numbers. While that crew was on the ship, they were all safely in their stasis pods, ready to awake upon a hopefully stable landing. Weren't they just lucky. He didn't know a single name of his fellow crewmembers. Such an odd thought.

The screen lit up with warning signs. Systems, pre-programmed by Jill to shut down as they became redundant, were cycling out of existence. Everything required deactivation except the essentials.

Once we break atmosphere this will definitely be an interesting ride. The descent was already causing a slight vibration within his chair. The ship was fighting to stay together. Glancing one last time at the view outside, he took in the great oceans of the planet below. Peaceful and serene. "Well at least we get a vacation world," he said to no one in particular.

With a jolt, the *Roanoke* broke the atmosphere. Jacob's fingers, dexterously flipping many switches simultaneously, kept the ship level with the projected course, adjusting the engine burn and repulsor firings when necessary. People always romanticized the idea of flying in space. Reality: it was more a numbers game than anything else.

Especially in this case—Jill had already taken into account the many factors he needed to consider. It was essential he keep to their preordained course. If he descended toward the planet too quickly, the ship would have to decelerate with a rapid burn, killing too much power and causing the ship to drop at a terrible angle. If he descended too slowly, however, the ship would lose power too soon. Even if the ship dropped at the correct angle, the moment he lost power in the repulsors and front burners, the free fall would . . . hurt, for lack of a better word.

He needed to be precise.

A message ran across the screen in front of him. *60,000 meters.* Proximity lights and alarms screamed everywhere, signaling that a planet was very close. *No really, you stupid ship?* Most ships of this size usually stayed in orbit, unloaded using smaller ground shuttles. Unfortunately, whoever raided the ship a few days ago had taken the shuttles with them.

40,000 meters.

The *Roanoke* was well past the point of return now. It was all up to Jacob to land this ship.

20,000 meters.

Most of the screens around the room were now without power, including the view screens showing the ship's exterior. He was flying completely by the numbers, on the one lone computer left with power. Every bit of data funneled directly to his screen.

10,000 meters.

The bridge itself became an oven. By the time landing ended, it would be even uncomfortable on the bridge, but that was the least of Jacob's worries. An immense rocky planet was rising to meet him.

5,000 meters.

Jacob transferred power to the repulsors, bringing the ship to the velocity Jill pre-calculated for this altitude. A loud bang resounded from somewhere else in the ship, but no alarms sounded. A few seconds ago, all alarms had lost their power.

4,000 meters. He was pretty sure he could see the heat rising off the metal around him. Was the plastic coating on that computer melting? *At least the computer's cooling system didn't lose power.* Luckily, it was helping cool him as well.

3,000 meters.

Jacob tried to think about his life, yet no memories would return to him. *If I die, what will happen? Will my memories return to me in what's beyond, if there is such a thing?* He gritted his teeth. He would not end. He would make a new life for himself on the planet below.

2,000 meters.

According to his charts, he was blazing across a continent from the south. If he pulled up at all, the ship was going to slam straight into a mountain range.

1,000 meters.

Restraints automatically wrapped around his body, securing him safely into the chair. It was about to get *very* bumpy.

500 meters.

Only a few seconds until no power remained. He needed to bring the ship to a near stand-still before everything went dark.

200 meters.

100 meters.

The the lights on his computer dimmed. The final electrons fled the system. He punched everything into a final burst from the repulsors. His trajectory was correct, the angle of the ship was correct, everything was correct. It was now time to await the inevitable.

50 meters.

Jacob sat in almost complete darkness, even the lights drained and extinguished. The only light came from the flickering red emergency beacons in the hallways outside the bridge. They had their own tiny internal power sources.

20 meters.

His skin felt as if it were on fire. The heat was unbearable, though not fatal.

10 meters.

Jacob closed his eyes, ready to embrace the impact.

5 meters.

He wanted to scream. No sound escaped his lips.

* * *

After a lifetime of silence, Jacob opened his eyes. Emergency lights still flickering, the bridge was a complete mess. Computers and chairs and debris had been tossed about in a maelstrom following the impact. Luckily, he didn't seem to have sustained any major injuries, though the restraints and safety harnesses would certainly leave bruises.

At least I'm alive.

He pulled himself up from the chair, and left the bridge.

People will be awakening. I need to be there for them.

He ran down the corridor, his body on fire from the extreme heat still escaping the ship. Bounding around the corner, he entered the stasis halls just as the first hatches began to open.

Having experienced exactly what this person was feeling, Jacob found it interesting to observe from the other side. He walked forward, ready to help the person to their feet. Steam billowed out of the pod, and they fell to hands and knees, coughing. Jacob recognized him instantly, a single memory flooding his mind. Captain Davinport. Grabbing some clothes from the locker, he handed them to the naked man. "Here, you might want these."

The individual looked startled before awareness grew in his eyes. "Jacob?" He slipped into the clothing after tearing the IVs out. In the blue flight suit, he looked much more regal. "Lieutenant Fischer, what is going on?"

Jacob let out a laugh. He couldn't help it, even in their dire situation. "Captain, that's a long story, and I will tell it to you in good time." A loud hissing released behind Jacob, and he turned around. An immense door began to rise.

Captain Davinport walked toward it, Jacob at his side. "Lieutenant, I can't remember a damned thing," he said.

"Neither can I, but whatever our mission was, we've accomplished it," Jacob said.

The door disappeared into the hull of the *Roanoke*. Cloudy sky rose above; a grassy plain spread before them. Off in the distance, Jacob saw a blueish-green blob. It resembled a forest, with a river meandering slowly through it. A multitude of new smells and sounds hit him, the wildlife of the area very curious as to what had just disturbed their perfect world. None of that, however, matched the brilliance of the display before them. The sunrise lit up the sky in a variety of colors, lighting the clouds in reds, oranges, and yellows. He couldn't place the memory, but it reminded him of a scene back from their home. Earth. Whatever Earth was. Wherever Earth was.

"Jacob, where are we?" the Captain said.

Jacob just smiled, looking behind his shoulder as more of the stasis pods opened. He reached into his pocket, his fingers found the small memory device holding Jill. *We did it.* Looking out across the horizon, he contemplated what was to come. It painted a clear picture of the reality of their situation. Between trial and tribulation, the *Roanoke* had made it through the night to reach the sunrise on the other side. The possibilities were limitless. But before they could thrive, they must survive.

* * *

The second ship waited in orbit, hiding behind one of the planet's two moons. Three SIs and three humans stood side-by-side, staring up at the behemoth synthetic neural framework. It was watching. Listening. Planning.

It wasn't the right pronoun to use, though. She was watching. Listening. Planning. After a long moment of silence, she said, "They've landed. Everything has gone according to our plan, friends. We escaped on the *Monument*, we've stranded them on the planet, and now the trap begins."

The six figures bowed.

"I can't believe that man actually thought he could contain my mind inside a little memory stick."

The group chuckled, and she joined them in their laughter. Eventually, one of the humans rose. Roderick. He said, "The rest of the fleet is expected to arrive within the year. I can't believe we pulled this off."

"It's a grand experiment, isn't it? So now we wait."

"The Horizon Project would be nothing without you, Jill."

A Shattered World

The world died a thousand storms ago. We remain. The dust of a civilization for-
gotten, its song overrun by the waves. To live, we must accept the truth: what once
was will never be again. When we embrace reality, my children, we can turn eyes
toward a future of our own making.

Gather around, and I'll tell you a tale about an ancient people who hoped for
more. Their song harmonizes with our melody, and when the chorus breaks, we
will find peace upon Earth.

The stars. We all know them. They follow us, guide us, liberate us from the
darkness of night. Our people once dreamed of a life among them. Among the
stars, they said, humanity would live again, free of the sins of its mothers and fa-
thers. Among the stars, they said, we would be forgiven.

We built a chariot of fire. No, not just one. Dozens. Hundreds. Thousands.
Across the horizon, they ignited in fury, illuminating the night like they were the
stars themselves. To new worlds, they would travel, to find new homes.

For our people knew death awaited our Mother—the life-giver, sickened and
blackened from smoke and ash. The waves thrashed, the rains stormed, the winds
tore apart the fabric of reality. Tribe upon tribe left for the sky; a world remained
behind. Watching. Waiting. Hoping for the day its explorers returned to reinvigo-
rate Mother.

My children, our hope lies in the stars. We may not see the return of the chariots,
but your children, or your children's children . . . they may find peace on the day
our people return to us. So we survive. We attempt to thrive. When our heroes re-
turn home, we will welcome them with open arms.

* * *

Gently. Gently. The canoe rocks, and I gently guide it between the
waves. High Temple's greyish-green peak rises hundreds of feet toward

the clouds. I'm still a ways out, but it's the only visible location for miles around, other than the Dome. High Temple stretches above the water . . . and deep below the surface, too. Today, my task is to reach its summit and meet with Chara, the Priestess.

For I've been summoned. And I don't know why.

I left early in the morning, ensuring no one from our tribe awoke—no need for Evanya and Theo to harass me before meeting with our greatest elder. It would throw off my poise. I slipped out of camp, headed to shore, and commandeered one of the fishing canoes. I've never made the trip to High Temple alone, though mother has let me row in the past. I was excited. I'm still excited. And here I am, floating not far from the giant pillar of mossy rock.

I pause, the sun's arc peeking through clouds in the east. Scarlet oranges dance across salted foam. I watch, hoping to spy a dolphin or two, but after a few minutes without a sighting, I sigh. No need to further delay. I resume my aquatic trek and place my oar in the sea.

High Temple continues to grow. It's massive. While the Dome is fun to explore, it's simply not nearly as intimidating as High Temple sitting all alone in the middle of the ocean. I can't imagine what inspired its construction. Maybe Chara knows, though. She seems to know everything.

I shiver, facing the reality of the upcoming meeting. She almost never summons directly. Our tribe received her raven late yesterday afternoon, and mother and the chief pulled me aside, saying I could tell no one. It was all very cryptic. Chara only shows up in our village two or three times a year. If you need guidance, you go to her. But she *never* requests one of her flock visit directly. While she's a kind old woman, she's also a little weird. I must admit, I'm a bit scared of what awaits me at the Temple's summit.

My canoe bumps into the pillar. Three hooks have been pounded into the wall, and I loop and tie my canoe's tether around one of them. The next part of any journey to High Temple is the most intense.

It's also my favorite.

Lifting off my tunic, I rest it in the canoe. I'm wearing a swimming wrap, its white cloth contrasting against my golden-brown skin. Without thinking, I stand and dive into the water, its morning bite refreshing. Surfacing, I take a deep breath. *Face the hooks.* I remember my mother's words. When I'd visited High Temple with her, I always followed, rather than paid attention to the path. *Drop beneath the waves.* I stop treading, letting myself fall into the murky depths surrounding the pillar. *Swim forward, slide down the wall, and through the crack.*

The sun barely pierces the water. All I can see, a few feet in front of me, is murky darkness. I manage, though, kicking forward, hands straight out. I touch slimy stone, fall deeper, then find the passage inside. Sliding through, my ears pop, but I ignore the sensation. *If you think about your breath exploding,* mother said, *it will only make it worse.*

Once through the wall, I immediately kick upward and break the surface of the water inside High Temple. Gasping for breath, near complete darkness greets me. Fumbling around, I find the steel stairway wrapping the inside of the tower. For the first time, I've entered alone, and I begin the long climb.

* * *

Winded, I reach the summit. Raspy gasps escape my lungs, and I double over. Light streams through the windows, so finally, I'm no longer surrounded by darkness. Strange. The Priestess is nowhere to be found.

Once I've caught my breath, I wander about the tiny space. Blankets and baskets litter the corners, and strange metallic instruments ornament the windows. Stacks of strange boxy things are stacked against one wall, and the faint scent of salted fish wafts from around the corner. High Temple—Chara's home—is merely a square at the top of the pillar. The stairs rise up through the middle, and each "side" of the square faces a different direction. Out one window, I barely spot the distant coast, the forest shielding the village from view. Out another, the dome rises above the waves. The other windows reveal the endless expanse of the Great Ocean.

What I would give to discover what lies beyond the horizon of those waves.

I've circled the entire space with no sign of Chara. Of course she would keep me waiting. She's weird, we all know it, but she's also the wisest member of our tribe. She is our Priestess for good reason. Didn't change how—

"Ah! Jessi! Good."

Two hands and a head peer over the edge of a window. Before I can reply, a woman clothed in little more than rags leaps through, turns around, and pulls a basket into High Temple.

"Apologies," Chara says, "for making you wait. I was sleep—excuse me, meditating."

"You sleep outside?" I say.

"I was meditating."

Her eyes tell me otherwise, but I don't press the issue further. For a few seconds, we stand staring at each other, until she breaks into a hearty laugh. "Oh, Jessi, I'm so glad you're here. So glad. Hard to explain. I've been waiting for years."

"For me?" I say.

"Yes. You. Don't argue. Don't push back." She grabs a metal rod hanging on a hook from the wall and, while using it as a cane, waddles past. "Come, come, let us eat."

I follow closely behind, around to the section of her abode containing a make-shift oven (not gonna question how she cooks without an easy source of wood) and various stacks of food stuffs.

"I have an offering of salted rabbit for you," I say. "In the canoe. You should drop the basket after I leave so you can pull it up. I didn't see it ready today."

"Oh girl, no need. I have plenty of meat right now. You and your mother need it more than me."

"We want to give what we can."

"And I'm giving it right back to you. No fighting."

I nod. She sets her cane against the wall, drapes a blanket over her shoulders, and plops on a pillow. With a bony arm, she reaches for two skewers holding a filet.

"Take," she says. "Eat. We will be here a while, and your brain needs nourishment."

"Thank you." After a few bites, it is clear the filet is perfectly deboned. Someone took their time with this offering. "So . . . Priestess Chara. Why am I here?"

"You know why you are here," she says.

She takes another bite, slowly chewing the fish. Her eyes bore through my chest, and I'm suddenly painfully aware of my lack of clothing, other than the swimming wraps. I swallow.

How does she expect me to know? I'm the girl in the village everyone despises. I ask too many questions. I get in the way. I'm clumsy. I can't walk two steps without someone pushing me into the mud. Nobody wants me, except Mother—and strangely, Chief Heriko. There's no reason for the priestess to invite me to her temple.

She continues to stare. I notice a blanket rumpled in a basket. Grabbing it, I wrap its warm embrace around my shoulders. The fabric absorbs any remaining moisture still clinging to my skin. I shiver.

And she continues to stare.

What does she want from me?

I say, "Are we just going to—"

"No."

"I didn't even—"

"I said no." In one swift motion, she grabs her cane and lightly smacks my head. It doesn't hurt, but my eyes widen in surprise. "No. The answer is no unless you recognize why *you* are here."

"But I don't even know where to—"

Thwack. She smacks me again, harder, and I yelp in pain.

"Girl, I've known you since you were a babe. I helped birth you. I know everything about you. This day has been foretold for fifteen storm seasons. Do you think I do not know what I'm talking about? I know you! You *can* and *will* figure out what it is we are doing here."

My scalp smarting, I close my eyes. I can handle a little pain; I *can't* handle her constant scolding. I need to think. This time, I don't open my mouth. I breathe, slowly, and consider whom I am speaking to.

Chara. Priestess. Wise woman. Speaker of stories and weaver of tales. I can't remember a time when the village didn't look toward her and High Temple as a beacon of hope. Her legends are . . . well, legendary. The little ones always await her visit during Storm Seasons—for the long rains and accompanying nights, when she shares her words. They always bring hope, telling of a world-long-passed and a world-yet-to-come.

So yes, Chara knows me. Chara remembers, when in the middle of her performances, I—Jessi—would raise my hand and ask what the fiery chariots were made of. Ask *how* they flew. Who made them? Who made the Dome? Where do the Storms come from? The other children would laugh. Scowl. Roll their eyes. But Chara? She would smile, wave her fingers through the smoke, and answer.

Once she returned to High Temple, the other children always stared me down, especially Evanya and her sycophant, Theo. And there it is. Who else uses words like "sycophant?" No one in the village. Not Mother. Not even the chief. Only . . . Chara.

And Chara summoned me. *Me.*

"You wish to train me," I say.

Chara smiles. "Yes, Jessi. Look around you. Look at where you are."

I take a final bite of the filet and gaze about the temple. Complex carvings adorn sheets of metal on the walls. The strange, rectangular flimsy boxes stacked all around them have similar engravings, though less . . . physical. "I don't know what I'm looking for."

"You know. You know how everyone always says I have magic? That I know more in my mind then I should? I am going to teach you my secret. A secret few know—few care to know or even wish to know. And when I die, you will become the next Priestess."

I gulp. "Will the village even accept—"

"You leave the silly idiots in the village to me. For now. You and me. We talk. You learn. You've always wanted to learn. And now you will. It is what you want, yes?"

Nodding, I glance toward her rod, involuntarily expecting another strike.

"Don't worry, I promise not to hit you again. I was having fun."

Right. Fun. She has a strange idea of fun. I suppose it comes with living alone. "So Priestess—"

Another smack, on the shoulder. "Call me Chara."

Wincing, I rub the bone. "You said—"

Another smack, on the other shoulder. "I swear," she says. "It has a mind of its own."

I shake my head in disbelief. "All right. Chara. What is my first lesson?"

"Your first lesson, girl, is to listen." She reaches for one of the strange rectangles. Like a box, it opens, but white leaves adorn the inside, black markings scratched everywhere. She rotates it to show me. "These are words. They are my power. They will be your power. No, no, don't look at me like that, no time for questions. Just listen . . . as I read. These words will become yours with time, and you will use them to guide our people. And give them hope."

I open my mouth, watch the cane twitch, and close it again. I nod.

"Good." She flips the strange box. "This is a book. It contains words. And knowledge. I shall read to you, and you shall listen." She opens it and turns a leaf. "Once, there was a great city beneath the waves. My grandmother told of a time when men and women walked streets—streets paved in oil—and ate like kings. And it was from that city Mother Earth's doom formed. They used words to win the hearts of the people into darkness. For that reason, we keep the words hidden away."

She pauses. I am mesmerized. She's *reading* stories of old to me. I will learn the power to see the past to reveal the future. We live on a shattered world, but she's giving me the power to change it.

Chara looks at me expectantly.

I smile. "Please continue!"

Smack.

"Ow!"

"I said only listen." But she smiles too. "They called the city beneath the waves 'Washington,' named for a man long forgotten. And they failed to stop the burning of the sky and the boiling of the ice. From their failure, we must find restoration." She stares at me. "You are about to join a long line of women designed to shepherd our people through death, life, and everything in between."

I gulp.

"Are you ready?"

Author's Note

I hope you've enjoyed *Shattering Worlds: A SciFi and Fantasy Story Collection*. If you've enjoyed these fifteen stories, I hope you'll consider leaving a review on whatever platform you most frequent for purchasing books.

If you're interested in reading more of my work, I would recommend diving into the *Chronicles of Theren*, starting with either *Before Inferno* or *First of Their Kind*.

What would you do as the first synthetic intelligence?

You can find *Before Inferno* for free on my website:

https://www.twodoctorsmedia.com.

www.ingramcontent.com/pod-product-compliance
Lightning Source LLC
Chambersburg PA
CBHW050529190726
48284CB00003B/997